"I'll do that later," she said. Then she left her hand on his arm and looked into his eyes, silently asking what he wanted next.

His eyes met hers, then his gaze shifted to her lips. She leaned closer, willing him to kiss her. His eyes darkened, and his grip on her arm tightened. She held her breath, waiting and wanting.

Then he took a step back. "I'd better go," he said, avoiding her gaze. "Thank you for dinner. I'll keep you posted on the case."

And then, before she could protest, he was gone. She stared after him, listening to his footsteps cross the floor, then the door close behind him.

The case. He meant Cash's disappearance. Maybe Basher's murder, too. The thing that had brought them together. Was it now the thing keeping them apart?

MISSING AT FULL MOON MINE

Cindi Myers

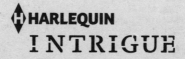

For Denise and Ron.

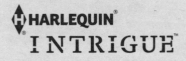

ISBN-13: 978-1-335-48946-3

Recycling programs
for this product may
not exist in your area.

Missing at Full Moon Mine

Copyright © 2022 by Cynthia Myers

All rights reserved. No part of this book may be used or reproduced in
any manner whatsoever without written permission except in the case of
brief quotations embodied in critical articles and reviews.

This is a work of fiction. Names, characters, places and incidents
are either the product of the author's imagination or are used fictitiously.
Any resemblance to actual persons, living or dead, businesses,
companies, events or locales is entirely coincidental.

This edition published by arrangement with Harlequin Books S.A.

For questions and comments about the quality of this book,
please contact us at CustomerService@Harlequin.com.

Harlequin Enterprises ULC
22 Adelaide St. West, 41st Floor
Toronto, Ontario M5H 4E3, Canada
www.Harlequin.com

Printed in U.S.A.

Cindi Myers is the author of more than fifty novels. When she's not plotting new romance story lines, she enjoys skiing, gardening, cooking, crafting and daydreaming. A lover of small-town life, she lives with her husband and two spoiled dogs in the Colorado mountains.

Books by Cindi Myers

Harlequin Intrigue

Eagle Mountain: Search for Suspects

Disappearance at Dakota Ridge
Conspiracy in the Rockies
Missing at Full Moon Mine

The Ranger Brigade: Rocky Mountain Manhunt

Investigation in Black Canyon
Mountain of Evidence
Mountain Investigation
Presumed Deadly

Eagle Mountain Murder Mystery: Winter Storm Wedding

Ice Cold Killer
Snowbound Suspicion
Cold Conspiracy
Snowblind Justice

Eagle Mountain Murder Mystery

Saved by the Sheriff
Avalanche of Trouble
Deputy Defender
Danger on Dakota Ridge

Visit the Author Profile page at Harlequin.com.

CAST OF CHARACTERS

Rebecca Whitlow—The arrival of her late brother's son has erased some of the loneliness in Rebecca's life, but his disappearance forces her to reexamine how far she has gone to protect herself from being hurt again.

Deputy Wes Landry—Wes came to Eagle Mountain to start over, but his attraction to Rebecca has him tempted to repeat mistakes that cost him in the past.

Cash Whitlow—The disappearance of this rising rock climbing star makes the whole town uneasy.

Basher Monroe—The murder of Cash's best friend casts suspicion on Cash.

Martin Kramer—The eccentric miner's claims of trespassers are dismissed as delusions, but could he have been the last person to see the missing climber?

Trey Allerton—Allerton has connections to several people involved in this case but maintains his innocence.

Bart Smith—The mysterious Smith spoke to Cash and Basher shortly before they disappeared, but now he has also vanished.

Chapter One

Rebecca Whitlow did not scare easy, but right now she was afraid. It was the kind of fear that took hold of her stomach and twisted, and kept her up nights with visions of everything terrible that might happen to the person she loved. When she did manage to sleep, fear filled her dreams with reminders of all the ways she had failed.

She pushed that anxiety back as she stepped into the Rayford County Sheriff's Department and looked around.

"May I help you?" A woman with short white hair and purple-rimmed glasses looked up from the desk in the center of the room.

Rebecca approached the desk. "I need to speak to someone about a missing person," she said.

"Who's missing?" the woman asked, not unkindly.

"My nephew. He lives with me." Rebecca looked around the lobby with its gray-painted walls, white-tile flooring and photographs of various men and women in uniform. "Is there someone I can talk to?"

"Have a seat and I'll get someone for you." The woman picked up a telephone at her elbow.

Rebecca moved to a row of straight-backed wooden chairs along one wall and sat, feeling a little like a schoolgirl waiting to see the principal. She hadn't done anything wrong, but she didn't know what to expect.

A door across the lobby opened and a uniformed thirtysomething man with dark curly hair emerged. He glanced toward the desk and the woman there nodded at Rebecca. She stood as he approached. "I'm Deputy Wes Landry," he said. "How can I help you?"

"My nephew is missing," she said. "He didn't come home last night, he isn't answering his cell phone and none of his friends have seen him."

"Come back here and I'll get some more information." He ushered her through the door to a desk in a room crowded with two other desks, a filing cabinet, a water cooler and many stacks of papers. He cleared some papers off a chair and indicated she should sit, then moved to sit behind the desk. He opened a notebook and picked up a pen. "What is your name and what is your nephew's name?"

"I'm Rebecca Whitlow, and my nephew is Cash Whitlow. He lives with me." She gave her address and phone number, and Cash's mobile phone number. "He's nineteen," she added. "He's a climber—a very good one. He works part-time as a climbing guide and has some professional sponsorships." She pressed her lips together to cut off the flow of words. She had so much she could say about Cash, but how much would this deputy want to hear?

Deputy Landry looked up from the pad of paper, into her eyes, and she felt the warmth and compassion of that gaze deep in her gut. He had blue eyes, the deep blue of a bird's feathers, with fine lines fanning from the corners that suggested he smiled a lot. The emotion behind the look—and the emotions it kindled in her—were so unexpected she let out a small gasp.

"Are you all right?" he asked, one eyebrow arched in question.

She looked down to her hands, clasped together in her lap. "I'm really worried about Cash," she said. "Since he moved in with me four months ago, he's never failed to come home at night, but he didn't come home last night. When I try to call him, the call goes straight to his voice mailbox. He isn't answering texts, either. I spoke to two of his best friends and they haven't heard from him." She forced herself to lift her head and look at the deputy again. It was important that he believe her, and that he take her seriously. "Because he's a climber, I worry he's been hurt, maybe in a remote location, and he's unable to summon help."

Deputy Landry nodded. "Do you know where he planned to climb yesterday?" he asked.

"No. I'm not even sure he was going to climb yesterday, though it's something he does several times a week. This morning I drove out to a couple of places I know about, but he wasn't there. His friends promised to look for him, too, but I thought it was time to get the sheriff's department involved."

"What about his job—you mentioned he works part-time as a guide. Did he work yesterday?"

She shook her head. "I called the outfitter he works for and they said he didn't work yesterday. Weekends are usually his busiest times, but I know he didn't have a client Saturday or Sunday. His boss hasn't heard from him, either."

"You say he's lived with you four months. Where did he live before that?"

"He was in California—Petaluma. He lived with his mother."

"Why did he decide to move in with you?"

"He committed himself to pursuing climbing professionally and Eagle Mountain has a big climbing community. And…and Cash's father, my brother, Scott, climbed here. Cash was only ten when Scott died, in a climbing accident. Cash wanted to live here, I think, as a way of getting closer to his father."

"What was your nephew's mood in the past few days?" the deputy asked.

"His mood?"

"Was he happy? Was he upset about anything?"

The band of tension around her head tightened. "He seemed happy, I guess. He was talking about taking a trip with some friends to Grand Teton to climb, maybe later this summer."

"So he wasn't depressed?"

"No. Why are you asking that?"

"I'm just trying to get a picture of him, that's all." He glanced down at the notepad again. "Did Cash have any history of trouble with drugs or alcohol?"

"Are you asking that because he's nineteen? Or because he's from California?"

"I'm asking because it's a question I would ask about any missing person," he said, his voice gentle.

She forced herself to relax, and to tell the truth, as much as she hated to reveal this side of her nephew to someone who didn't know him. "Cash has struggled with addiction in the past," she said. "Heroin and pills. But he completed an in-patient rehab program six months ago and I swear he's been clean since."

"Relapses aren't uncommon," Deputy Landry said.

"I know that." She forced herself to lower her voice. "It's something I'm always watching for, but I swear, there haven't been any signs. Cash is focused on climbing. It's something he has a real talent for. He can have a good future in the sport, but he knows he has to be sober to pursue that dream." She leaned toward him. "Don't dismiss him as just another addict who's off on a bender," she said. "That's not who he is. I know something is really wrong."

"I promise I take your worries seriously," he said.

His gaze didn't waver and his reassurance made her feel calmer. She sat back. "Thank you."

"Do you have a recent picture of Cash?" he asked.

"Yes." She opened her purse and took out a colored flyer. A smiling Cash stood in front of a rock face, climbing rope slung over one shoulder. "This is a flyer for a climbing clinic he taught at last month."

"Climbing phenom Cash Whitlow," the deputy read. "So he's well-known enough other climbers would recognize him?"

"A lot of them would, I think. Especially if they live around here. He's gotten a lot of attention in the media."

"So some people might be jealous of him—someone so young and I take it relatively new to the sport getting so much press?"

A chill washed over her. "Are you saying you think someone might have…hurt him?"

"I'm trying to consider every possibility," he said. "Do you have any reason to suspect foul play?"

"None. Cash has never mentioned any threats, or even anyone acting jealous of him." She bit her lip, struggling again for composure. "You'd have to know him to understand, but Cash is someone who is very hard to dislike. He's very charming and he has a sweetness about him…" Her voice trailed off, and she tried again. "You probably think I'm just a doting aunt, but if you talk to his friends, you'll see I'm right."

The deputy picked up his pen again. "Give me the names of some of his friends and how I can reach them, if you know. That will be a good place to start."

She gave him the names she knew and where they worked or where they would be likely to be climbing, as well as the name and number of the guide service Cash worked for.

"Did he have a love interest?" the deputy asked.

"Do you mean a girlfriend?"

"Or a boyfriend?"

"He wasn't dating anyone," she said. "He's flirted with girls, but he told me he didn't have time to get serious about anyone right now."

"Does he have a car?"

"Yes. He drives an old gray Toyota Tacoma with a topper over the bed."

"How old?"

She laughed. "Old. I think it's a 1995 or 1996. But it runs well."

"Does he camp out in it?"

"Sometimes. Especially if he wants to get an early start on a climb. But if he's going to be out late, he has always called me before. And he's never not responded to my texts."

The deputy nodded. "There are a lot of areas around here with no cell service. Especially in canyons where he might be climbing."

"Yes. That's why I'm so worried. If he's hurt, he wouldn't even be able to call for help."

"Is there anything else you think I need to know about Cash?"

She thought a moment, then said, "He's a good kid, but he's just a kid. He has a reckless streak."

"What do you mean?"

"He takes risks when climbing. It's one of the things that makes him so good—that lack of fear. But he climbs alone sometimes, which everyone—

even he—agrees isn't the safest choice. He thinks he's invincible—like most nineteen-year-olds, I guess."

"I'll start with the guide shop and his friends," the deputy said. "We'll put the word out for everyone to be on the lookout for him, and we'll ask for their help checking out places he might have climbed. We'll put out a bulletin with Cash's picture and a description of him and of his car. Maybe someone will see the vehicle and that will help us narrow the search area."

"I thought I would print flyers with that information," she said. "I could post them around town and give them to other climbers."

"That's a good idea." He stood and she rose also. He handed her a business card. "If you think of anything else, or if you learn anything—and of course, if you hear from Cash, call me," he said. "Anytime."

"Thank you."

He glanced down at his notes again. "If I need to reach you, is the number you gave me the best contact?"

"Yes. But I work weekdays, eight to six, at the Eagle Mountain Medical Clinic. If for some reason I don't answer when you call my cell, you can try that number."

"What do you do at the clinic?"

"I'm the office manager."

"You're not working today?"

"I took a personal day. I wouldn't have been able to concentrate, worrying about Cash."

"I'll call you right away if we learn anything," he said.

"Thank you. I just… I feel so helpless." The words

burst out of her, and she felt a hot flush on her cheeks. This officer didn't care about her personal emotions.

"Not knowing what's going on with someone you love is always hard," he said. "But remember, you're not alone now. A lot of people are going to be looking for Cash, wanting to help him. If he's out there, we'll do everything in our power to find him."

He touched her shoulder—a light brush of his fingers, but she felt the warmth like a caress. She carried the heat of that moment with her out into the lobby and back to her car. Then she sat for a long moment, collecting her thoughts, which were a tangle of worry about Cash, and confusion over why she had reacted so strongly to Deputy Wes Landry. She interacted with men all day long, some of them as handsome and masculine as the deputy, but she was usually so sure of herself—what she wanted, who she liked. But the deputy had thrown her completely off-kilter.

"Was that Rebecca Whitlow just leaving?" Deputy Shane Ellis asked as Wes was finishing up his notes about Cash Whitlow. Shane stood in the doorway of the squad room, coffee mug in hand.

"It was," Wes said. "Do you know her?"

"She works at the clinic with Lauren."

Shane's girlfriend, Lauren Baker, was a nurse practitioner, Wes remembered. "She came in to file a missing person's report on her nephew, Cash Whitlow," Wes said.

"The climber?" Shane moved to the desk across from Wes.

"Do you know him?" Wes asked.

"I know of him. There was an article about him in the local paper about a month ago. He's apparently an up and coming star in the sport. Didn't you see it?"

"Guess I missed it." Wes had sworn off newspapers when he worked in St. Louis, where he found the reporting either sensationalized, depressing or both. Maybe small-town publications were different.

"You need to keep up," Shane said with a grin. Then his expression sobered. "So what's up with Cash now?"

"Ms. Whitlow is worried he's gone off climbing by himself and been hurt. He didn't come home last night and he's not answering calls or texts. She spoke with a couple of his friends and they haven't heard from him, either."

"He's taking a big risk, climbing alone," Shane said. "If he did fall in some of these remote canyons, it could be weeks before someone finds him."

"That's what Ms. Whitlow is afraid of." Wes shoved his chair back and rose. "I'm going to talk to Cash's boss and a few more of his friends, then put out an APB on his car with a description of him. If we're lucky, he just stayed out late with a friend his aunt doesn't know about."

"He's young, right?" Shane asked.

"He's nineteen." *And a former addict.* He'd keep that information confidential for now, but if they didn't find the young man hurt in a climbing accident or out with friends, they had to consider he was back on drugs. He might have left town altogether, gotten in trouble with a supplier or even overdosed. There was a long list of the ways someone could get in serious trouble with drugs.

"Then that's probably it," Shane said. "He'll be mortified when he finds out his aunt came to us."

"Maybe. But I'd rather do too much than too little." He knew too well the consequences of inaction.

He walked down the hall to the sheriff's office and knocked. Sheriff Travis Walker looked up from his computer screen. "Hey, Wes." Lanky and handsome in a way that recalled big-screen cowboys, Travis had recruited Wes to join the Rayford County force when he heard his friend was looking to leave the big city. He hadn't questioned Wes's reasons for wanting to quit St. Louis, merely suggested the small town of Eagle Mountain as a change of scenery where he'd have a chance to deal with all kinds of cases and work independently at a slower pace. He had persuaded Wes that this rural sheriff's department could use an officer with Wes's experience.

"Rebecca Whitlow just filed a missing person's report on her nephew, Cash," Wes said. He filled the sheriff in on the details and added, "If he is in the habit of climbing alone, then an accident seems likely, but she also shared that Cash is only six months out of drug rehab."

"We don't have a huge drug problem in Rayford

County, but it is here," Travis said. "There have been a few indications of a new supplier in the area, but nothing concrete. If Cash doesn't turn up at the climbing hot spots, I can give you some names of people to question, places to look."

"Thanks. I hope it doesn't come to that."

"Let me know if you need help with anything. You're still getting familiar with people here and I'll smooth the way if you run into any resistance." Travis's family had lived in the area for several generations and the sheriff seemed to know everyone.

"Thanks. I'll let you know if I need anything." He left the office and climbed into the black-and-white SUV that had been assigned to him. He'd start at the guide shop where Cash worked part-time, then head out to Caspar Canyon, where he'd seen climbers on the sandstone canyon walls almost every time he drove past.

On his way to the guide shop, he passed Eagle Mountain Medical Clinic. Every parking spot in front of the storefront clinic was filled. Since Rebecca Whitlow wasn't working, he wondered what she was doing now. Maybe she'd gone to the print shop to order the flyers she'd mentioned. Even in her anxiety, she had the suppressed energy of someone who was used to action. She hadn't delayed in coming to the sheriff's office to report her concerns about her nephew, and she had already started the search process, talking to his friends and driving to areas where she knew he climbed. She wasn't going to sit back and let others do all the work.

That kind of personality could be both a help and a hindrance to police work, Wes knew from experience. In St. Louis he had had to deal with parents and other relatives who second-guessed his every action or who interfered with investigations. Would Rebecca be like that?

He didn't think so. Or maybe he didn't want to believe it of her. He wasn't ready to think too much about the emotions that had arisen when he'd first looked into her warm brown eyes, a mixture of sexual attraction and personal connection that wasn't the most welcome combination when dealing with someone involved in a case. Moving to a small town must have led him to subconsciously let down the barriers that kept his personal and professional lives firmly separated. The lovely Ms. Whitlow just happened to come along at the wrong time.

Well, he'd deal with it. In any case she probably had a partner who wrestled steers for a living and was insanely jealous. He wouldn't blame the man.

Wes parked in front of Colorado Mountain Guides and entered. Displays of boots, packs and other climbing gear filled the front window and crowded the walls and aisles of the small space. As Wes moved toward the counter at the rear of the store, a muscular man with a shaved head and a silver goatee emerged from a back room. "What can I do for you, Deputy?" he asked.

"I'm looking for Cash Whitlow," Wes said. "I understand he guides for you."

"You're the second man this week who's been in here looking for Cash, but you don't look as angry as the first one."

"Oh? Who was that?"

"He didn't leave his name, but I can tell you he was riled up. Don't know about what, but he threatened to kill the boy if he saw him again."

Chapter Two

Suddenly the disappearance of Cash Whitlow sounded a lot more serious. "When was this?" Wes asked.

"Yesterday afternoon." The big man leaned close, elbows propped on the counter. "I didn't catch your name. Are you new with the sheriff's department?"

"Wes Landry." Wes handed over one of his cards. "I've been with Rayford County a couple of months." Seven weeks, but who was counting?

"Doug Michelson." The big man stuck out a beefy hand. His handshake was firm but not crushing, for which Wes was grateful.

"Back to the man who was looking for Cash," Wes said. "What time was he here, exactly?"

"A little after two o'clock. He didn't say good afternoon or how do you do or anything. He just asked if Cash was here. I told him no and he asked—demanded, really—to know when he'd be in. I told him Cash doesn't actually work in the store. When someone needs a guide, I pass on Cash's information to them and the two of them arrange things between them. I handle the payments and take a twenty percent cut. That way Cash doesn't have to handle the accounting because, let's face it, most of these rock rats aren't into paperwork."

"What did the man say—exactly?"

"He said, *Next time you see Cash, you tell him I'm going to kill him if he doesn't mind his own business.* Then I asked him for his name and he said, *Cash knows who I am,* and left."

"What did he look like?"

Michelson rested his chin on his clasped hands. "I can tell you what he looked like, but here's the thing— I don't think it was what he *really* looked like."

"What do you mean?"

"He was wearing mirrored sunglasses and a big straw hat and I think a wig. A really bad black wig, like you'd buy for a Halloween costume."

"He was wearing a disguise?" Wes asked.

"I think so, yeah."

Wes took a notebook and pen from his pocket. "Tell me what you can."

Michelson straightened. "He was a white guy, about six-two, good build, like he worked out. He had on baggy jeans and a loud Hawaiian shirt—lime green with alligators and flowers on it. I think that was probably part of the disguise, too."

"Any rings?" Wes asked. "Earrings? Tattoos? What kind of shoes?"

Michelson shook his head. "I didn't notice any jewelry or ink, and I didn't pay attention to his shoes, either. Sorry."

"Do you have a security camera that might have gotten an image of him?"

"Nope."

"What about his car? Did you see what he was driving?"

"No. He headed down the sidewalk, east, I think."

Wes made note of this. You never knew what information might turn out to be useful. "When was the last time you saw or spoke to Cash?" he asked.

"I saw him last Thursday when he stopped by to pick up a check. I spoke to him on the phone Saturday morning, about a guy who wanted to book a guide for next month when he's in town."

"Did Cash talk about going out of town or anything like that?"

Michelson shook his head. "No. He sounded his usual self. We talked about climbing, and that's about it."

"Do you have any idea where he might be right now?"

"He lives with his aunt, Rebecca Whitlow. She called here this morning first thing, asking if I'd seen Cash. She sounded kind of worried. I didn't tell her about the man who was here yesterday looking for Cash. I didn't want to upset her. Have you talked to her?"

Wes nodded. "I have. Anyone else?"

"All the local climbers know Cash, you could ask

them." His expression darkened. "Why are you look-ing for Cash? What's he done?"

"He hasn't done anything. His aunt hasn't heard from him in a couple of days and she's worried he might have gone climbing by himself and been hurt."

"One of the first rules in climbing is to not do it alone, but it happens all the time."

"Why is that, do you think?"

"Oh, there's always a good excuse." Michelson waved his hand in the air. "A guy is anxious to do a climb and his buddy can't go. Or he wants to be the first to climb a new route and wants to keep his plan secret. Or he just likes being up there alone. I get it, but that doesn't mean it's smart."

Wes tucked the notebook and pen back in his pocket. "Let me know if you hear anything from Cash or about him."

Michelson nodded. "Will do. And I hope you find him, and that he's okay. As aggravating as he could be sometimes, he's a good kid, and a heck of a climber."

Wes left the shop, puzzling over the man in the Ha-waiian shirt and straw hat. He sounded like a character in a bad melodrama, right down to the clichéd threats. Was Cash pulling some elaborate prank on the cops? But that would mean Rebecca Whitlow was involved and he didn't want to believe that of her. Her distress over her missing nephew had seemed genuine.

He asked about the man and Cash at other busi-nesses along the street. None of the shop owners had seen the man in the Hawaiian shirt and straw hat, but they all knew Cash and dubbed him a good kid.

"Did you know him well?" Wes asked the manager of Mo's Tavern, a white-bearded man in a flat tweed cap who introduced himself as George.

"He and his friends come in here to eat a couple of times a week," George said. "Maybe have a few beers. Not Cash—he never drank, that I saw. Except those energy drinks in a can—he likes those. But nothing alcoholic. Not that I'd serve him. I know he's under age."

Wes handed George his card. "If you see him, let me know. He hasn't gotten in touch with his aunt and she's worried about him."

"Rebecca? Sweet lady."

"What can you tell me about her?"

George's eyes narrowed. "I told you—she's a sweet lady."

"Would you say she and Cash have a good relationship?"

"What are you trying to imply?"

"I'm not implying anything. Maybe they had an argument and Cash is lying low for a few days to cool off, or he resented having to live by her rules and moved in with a friend."

George shook his head. "Nothing like that. I'd say he thinks the world of her, and she feels the same about him. I saw her at the climbing festival last month, cheering him on when he was competing, and he sent her flowers on Mother's Day—he was eating lunch in here when she came and found him and thanked him and gave him a big hug. So if you think she had anything to do with him disappearing, you need to think again."

"I'm not drawing any conclusions right now," Wes said. "Just asking a lot of questions and gathering as much information as I can."

"You should talk to Basher Monroe. He's in here with Cash a lot. They had lunch in here, just the two of them, on Sunday." His expression sobered. "Come to think of it, they had their heads together, in what looked like a pretty serious conversation."

"Any idea what they were talking about?" Wes asked.

George shook his head. "No. We were busy and I didn't have time to stand around eavesdropping."

"Know where I can find Basher?"

"He hangs out at that area along County Road Five, by the creek. There's a stretch in there with some waterfalls and sheer rock faces where people climb. Basher drives an old ambulance he's converted into a kind of camper. He lives out of it, I think."

Wes made note of this. "Thanks."

"Cash is a good kid and I hope nothing's wrong with him," George said. "I'll keep my ears open and let you know if I hear anything."

Wes returned to his SUV, mulling over all he'd heard. Cash was a good kid. Cash didn't drink. He had a good relationship with his aunt.

But nobody had seen him or heard from him in more than twenty-four hours. As much as Wes hoped he'd find the kid staying with a friend or climbing in an area with no cell service, he couldn't help sharing Rebecca's feeling that something wasn't right with this picture. And if they were right and Cash was in trouble, the longer he went unfound, the worse things might turn out to be.

REBECCA LEANED FORWARD and clutched the steering wheel tighter as she neared her house, only to sag with the weight of disappointment as she pulled into the empty driveway. She had hoped so strongly that Cash would be there, with some story of having dropped his phone on a night out with friends, or that he'd been stranded by car trouble in an area with no service. Her relief at seeing him would have overwhelmed any embarrassment she might have felt over having to call Deputy Landry to tell him to call off the search.

Walking into her empty house now, after she had asked the sheriff's department to help, made the reality of Cash's disappearance all the more dire. She wasn't the sort of person who dwelled on worst-case scenarios or who expected disaster at every turn, but fear for her nephew had lodged itself like a bone in her throat.

All she could do now was try to swallow past that fear and work on the flyer the deputy had agreed she should make and distribute.

She had dreaded going to the sheriff, worried the authorities would dismiss her as worried over an irresponsible teen who was probably out with friends, or worse, that they would focus on Cash's history of addiction and not the strength he had shown in overcoming those problems. But Deputy Landry had taken her complaint seriously. He understood the danger Cash might be in, and while he had been concerned about Cash's former drug use (he had to be, she acknowledged), he hadn't made it the focus of his efforts to find the young man. Or, at least, he hadn't admitted so to her.

She went to the desk in the corner of the living room and switched on her laptop, then headed to the kitchen, intending to make a cup of tea. But before she could fill the kettle her gaze came to rest on the photo in a magnetic frame on the front of the refrigerator— a young man in a climbing harness festooned with coils of rope, quickdraws, sling, belays and a chalk bag, climbing helmet shoved up to reveal a tangle of messy blond curls and a grin so broad and joyful it seemed to her the very image of happiness.

Though the resemblance to Cash was strong, this young man was actually her brother, Scott, Cash's father. She had taken that photograph of him here in Eagle Mountain, up on Dakota Ridge, eleven months before he was killed in a climbing accident not far from where this picture had been taken. She had hung the photo on the refrigerator, where she could see it every day, shortly after Scott's funeral, as a reminder that he had died doing what he loved most. Though he had been taken too young, deprived of seeing his son grow up, Scott would have had no regrets about how his end came.

But please, God, don't let Cash be taken the same way. Rebecca didn't think she could bear it.

Instead of making tea, she left the kitchen and went down the hall to Cash's room. She had searched the room earlier this morning, desperate for some clue as to where Cash might be, but had found nothing. No drugs—which was good—but very little else. A few clothes, some climbing magazines and a phone charger. The charger worried her—did he have one in his car? No diary, no books, no computer or letters or cryptic notes about planned meetings or get-togethers. Except for a pair of slippers by the bed and dirty clothes on the closet floor, the room looked much as it had when Rebecca had used it as a guest room. "I should tell him to put some posters or pictures on the wall when he gets back," she said out loud as she moved into the room.

Talking to herself probably wasn't a good sign, but the house felt so empty. Amazing how full one active teen had made it seem in the four months Cash had lived here.

She went to the open closet and gathered up the pile of dirty clothes. Washing them would give her something to do. She checked the pockets of the pants and shook out the shirts, then froze and stared at the dark stain down the front of one of the shirts—dark brown and stiff.

With a feeling of dread churning her stomach,

she brought the garment to her nose. Was that a faint metallic odor? She dropped the shirt on the bed and stared at it, telling herself she was mistaken. The stain was barbecue sauce, or ketchup.

But she worked in a medical clinic. She had seen that kind of stain too often not to recognize its origin.

But why was there a bloodstain on the front of Cash's shirt? And whose blood was it?

Chapter Three

Rebecca left a message for Deputy Landry to call her, but she didn't hear from him until he showed up at her house after six that evening. She answered his knock, heart racing, and stood frozen for a moment, searching his face, trying to read his expression. "Have you found out anything?" she asked, torn between wanting news and fearing the worst.

"I haven't found Cash," he said. "But I have some more questions and I got your message. May I come in?"

"Of course." She stepped back and held the door open wider. A stack of the flyers she had made sat on a small table by the door and she picked up one and handed it to him. "I made these and put some up around town," she said.

The flyer featured the picture of Cash from the climbing poster, with details about his height, weight, and hair and eye color, as well as a description of his truck. *Contact the sheriff's department or Rebecca Whitlow with any information*, she had printed in bold letters across the bottom of the flyer, along with her phone number. "No one has responded yet," she said. "I'll put more out tomorrow."

"That's good." He returned the flyer to her. "You said in your message you'd found something I should see?"

"Right. It may be nothing, but I thought you should see it." She moved to the kitchen, where a plastic bag containing the bloody shirt lay on the counter. She hadn't been sure what else to do with it. "I searched Cash's room again when I got home from talking to you," she said. "I didn't really find anything, but when I gathered up his dirty laundry from the closet, there was this." She handed him the bag.

He opened it and looked inside, then pulled out the shirt.

"I can't be positive, but I thought that stain looks like blood," she said. She was jittery with nerves. What if that was just a food stain or oil from working on his truck? But it hadn't smelled like those things, and there was so much of it.

Deputy Landry pushed the shirt back into the bag. "I'll have this tested," he said. "When you last saw Cash, was he hurt?"

"No. He was fine."

"When was that?"

"At supper, Sunday. He went out again after that, but I heard him come in late—around midnight. I woke up and heard him in the hallway. I called out to him and he said hello and apologized for waking me.

He slept in the next morning, and when I came home from work, he wasn't here. I texted him and he didn't answer but I wasn't worried until he didn't come home last night at all. And when he still didn't answer my calls and texts, and none of his friends knew where he was, I decided to contact the sheriff's department."

Landry nodded, and put the bag with the shirt in it back on the counter. "We've got teams out searching Caspar Canyon and other known climbing areas," he said. "Tomorrow we've arranged to have a helicopter do an aerial search."

"That's great." With so many people looking, surely they would find Cash.

"Why don't we sit down?" he said. "I need you to fill in a few blanks in the information I've managed to gather."

"Of course." She led the way into the living room, to the sofa.

She sat at one end and he settled on the other and took out his notebook. "I talked to Doug Michelson at Colorado Mountain Guides," he said. "He hasn't seen or heard from Cash in a few days, but that isn't unusual. Apparently Cash only has contact with him when someone wants to hire a climbing guide."

"I know Cash is busier with that at some times than others," she said. "But he's not really interested in full-time work. He devotes most of his time to training and climbing. It's a different lifestyle from most people, but he's able to travel and do what he loves, and he has sponsors who help with expenses and gear."

"Mr. Michelson told me a man came into his shop yesterday afternoon, looking for Cash. He described him as about six foot two inches, with a muscular build. He wore a straw hat and a loud Hawaiian shirt and had dark curly hair, but Michelson thought that might have been a wig. Does that sound familiar to you?"

She stared, trying to make sense of his words. "A wig? Was this man in some kind of costume?"

"I don't know. Maybe he was trying to disguise his appearance. Michelson said he was angry. Can you think of anyone who might have been angry at Cash and looking for him?"

"No."

"When Cash moved here from California, was he moving away from someone or something?" Landry asked.

"No. Nothing like that," she said. "He came here for the climbing." She leaned toward him, sensing there was a lot he wasn't telling her. "Why was this man angry with Cash? Did he say?"

"He told Michelson Cash would know who he was and he threatened him if Cash didn't mind his own business."

"That doesn't make sense. What would Cash have been doing that made him so angry?"

"I don't know, and neither did Michelson. You can't think of anything?"

"No." None of this made any sense. "How did the man threaten Cash? What did he say?"

"According to Michelson, he said, *Next time you see Cash, you tell him I'm going to kill him if he doesn't mind his own business*."

Dizziness washed over her and she might have swayed. Landry leaned over and gripped her arm. "It may have been an idle threat. The kind of thing someone says in the heat of the moment."

She nodded and wet her dry lips. "Or maybe it wasn't."

"I promise you, we're taking this seriously." He stood. "I'd like to see Cash's room."

She stood also and took him to the room down the hall from her own. "I've looked through it twice now and haven't found anything except that shirt. There really isn't much to look through."

The deputy stood in the doorway and surveyed the room, his eyes traveling over the unmade bed and simple dresser. "Does Cash have a computer?" he asked after a long moment.

"No. He uses his phone. It's not here, so I'm sure he has it with him, though he left the charger plugged in, on top of the dresser.

"Is anything else missing? I don't see any climbing gear."

"He kept all that in his truck."

He nodded and moved over to the dresser, and studied the few items on top—the phone charger, some change, a half pack of gum and a tube of lip balm.

Rebecca came to stand beside him. "Deputy Landry,

how long have you worked in law enforcement?" she asked.

He looked at her, his gaze warm yet unnerving, but she forced herself to meet it. "Call me Wes," he said. "We're going to be seeing a lot of each other until Cash is found. And I was with the St. Louis Police Department for fourteen years."

"All right, Wes." The name was as solid and steady as him. "You can call me Rebecca. Have you worked many missing persons cases?"

"Quite a few."

"Then you must have some instincts about these things. What do you think is going on?"

He was silent so long she wondered if she had offended him. "Please, I'm not questioning your abilities," she said. "But I need you to be honest with me."

"Something isn't right," he said. "It feels like we're missing an important part of the story. The friends of Cash who I was able to talk to weren't aware of any new places he intended to climb, and they swear they haven't seen him or his truck in the past two days. I'm still trying to locate someone called Basher Monroe. The manager of Mo's Tavern said he was a friend of Cash's—another climber who lives in an old ambulance he's converted to a camper."

"I know the person you're talking about," she said. "Or rather, I know of him. I've never met him." She frowned. "I wasn't aware he and Cash were good friends."

"George, the manager, said they ate at Mo's pretty often."

She blew out a breath. "Cash probably has a lot of friends I don't know about."

"Then there's the man in the loud shirt and the wig," Wes said. "There's something so off about him."

"I'm sure Cash never mentioned anyone like that," she said.

"Is Cash the type to play pranks?" Wes asked. "Would he set up something like this, not meaning to alarm anyone, but as an elaborate joke?"

"No!" She shook her head vehemently. "Cash is really quiet. He's very serious—too serious sometimes, I think. He isn't the extroverted jokester. You might even call him socially awkward—about everything except climbing. He's a different person on rock or ice, competent and very sure of himself."

"So climbing is pretty much his whole focus."

"I don't want you to think he's one dimensional." She struggled to find the words to describe her nephew. "He's very focused on becoming the very best climber he can be. Partly because he loves the sport, but also as a means to do even bigger things. He and I talked about that a lot. He really wants to work with kids, maybe troubled kids, to teach them climbing and about the outdoors—maybe at some kind of camp or outdoor school. Climbing is a pathway to that."

He nodded. "You're giving me a much better picture of him. Thank you."

They returned to the kitchen and he collected the

bag with the shirt. "I'll be in touch," he said. "We're going to do our best to figure out what's going on."

"I have faith in you," she said.

The words seemed to pain him, and he shook his head. "Have faith in Cash instead. He's obviously a strong young man."

Yes, she thought when Wes had left. Cash was a strong young man. But if she had to depend on someone, she would choose a man of experience as well as strength. Someone like Wes Landry.

INSTEAD OF GOING HOME, Wes drove down County Road Five, hoping to find Basher Monroe. The sun was sinking fast behind the trees, casting the area beneath the limestone cliffs into deep shadow. The parking area was deserted and as Wes drove slowly through the area, he saw no vehicles or people.

Past the climbing area, the gravel forest service road narrowed, with dark evergreens crowding in on either side. The road became more rutted, and Wes had to slow his speed even more to negotiate the ruts. It didn't look as if this part of the road got much use.

He was looking for a place to turn around when he spotted a break in the trees. He eased his SUV into the space, intending to back out, but stopped when his headlights flashed off something metallic. He hit the switch for his spotlight and lit up the back bumper of a vehicle—something square and boxy, like a van.

Or an ambulance. He pulled out a large flashlight and, leaving the SUV running and the spotlight on, he moved toward the vehicle. As he walked closer, he could make out the faded red stripe all the way around the vehicle, the traditional marking for an ambulance. The vehicle was nosed into a small clearing some fifty yards off the road, mostly hidden by a thick screen of brush. Wes stopped ten yards away and called out, "Hello! Anyone home?"

No answer or even movement from the vehicle. No lights shone in the rear windows, which were covered in some kind of reflective material. "Hello!" Wes called again.

Here, deeper in the trees, it was almost full darkness. Somewhere in the distance, a coyote yipped and another group answered from farther away. A branch popped beneath Wes's boot and he froze, waiting and listening, but heard nothing except his own labored breathing and the rustle of a breeze high overhead.

He reached the back of the ambulance and shone the light along the driver's side. The driver's door stood open, though he could see nothing in the blackness within. "Hello!" he called again, but without much hope he'd receive an answer. Had Basher— or whoever drove this vehicle—fled into the woods when Wes had discovered his hiding place? He hadn't heard anyone running away, but maybe the throb of the SUV's engine and the thick duff on the forest floor had obscured the sound of running footsteps.

He took a deep steadying breath and moved forward. The beam of his flashlight illuminated the empty driver's seat, the upholstery patched in several places with duct tape, more tape around the steering wheel. A passage between the front seats provided access to the rear of the vehicle. Wes leaned in and caught the funk of stale marijuana smoke and cooking grease. He played the beam of light across a counter with a propane stove, a water jug cradled in a metal rack and a small dinette. The rear of the camper seemed to consist of a bunk, blankets piled on top of the mattress.

He froze, his light trained on the bunk, as he realized there was something beneath the blankets. Or rather someone. He fixed the beam on one bare foot poking out from under the covers. "Hey!" he called. Then louder, "Basher, is that you? Wake up!"

The occupant of the bunk didn't move. A cold chill crept up Wes's spine as he continued to stare at the bare foot, the flesh so white in the bright light. He heaved himself into the vehicle and climbed over the driver's seat and into the back. By the time he reached the bunk, he knew what he would find. He used the light to fold back the corner of the blankets farthest from that bare foot.

A big man with dreadlocks wet with blood stared up at him with lifeless eyes, his mouth open in a last cry of horror.

Chapter Four

After Wes left, Rebecca picked up her phone. She needed to let Cash's mom know what was going on, though she'd been putting off the call as long as possible. She had never been entirely comfortable with her sister-in-law. Scott's death and Pamela's decision to move back to California hadn't brought them any closer. But for Cash's sake, Rebecca had done her best to maintain contact, though their infrequent phone conversations often felt stilted.

"Hello, Rebecca." As usual Pamela's voice was cool when she answered the call.

"Hi, Pamela. How are you doing?"

"I'm fine. Did you need something?" That was Pamela—no time for polite chitchat.

"Have you spoken to Cash lately?" Rebecca asked.

"No. Why? What has he done now?"

Why did she assume Cash had done anything? "I'm worried about him," Rebecca said. "He left the house sometime after I left for work yesterday morning and no one has heard from him since. I was hoping he'd mentioned his plans to you."

"Cash doesn't tell me his plans. And I'm not surprised he didn't tell you, either. He's probably gone off with friends. He'll come back when he's out of money."

"None of his friends know where he is," Rebecca said. "I'm worried he went climbing and got hurt. Has he talked to you about exploring a new area?"

"I told you, we don't talk." Pamela's voice had a sharp edge. "Especially not about climbing. I made it clear that I didn't approve of him going to Colorado. He would be much better off going into therapy than trying to work out his daddy issues hanging from bare rock. And you haven't helped matters by supporting him in this foolishness."

Rebecca flinched. Even over the phone she felt the force of Pamela's anger. "I don't think either one of us could stop Cash once he made up his mind," she said. "At least by giving him a place to stay, I could make sure he was eating and had somewhere to sleep besides his truck."

"But you don't know where he is now, so you can't say things worked out, can you?"

"Pamela—" Rebecca began.

"I'm sorry. That was harsh. But you haven't spent the last ten years dealing with Cash. I have. You don't know how many nights I lay awake worrying about him or how many miles I put on my car driving around looking for him when he was out partying or trying to score drugs. I thought when he finally admitted he needed help and went into rehab that things would be better, but instead of going back to school and getting a job and pulling his life together, he decided to run off to Colorado and follow in his father's footsteps. Fine. I'm done tying myself into knots fretting over his foolish choices." Her voice broke, and Rebecca wondered if she was crying.

"I know you did everything you could for Cash," Rebecca said softly. "I can only begin to imagine how hard it was for you. But I don't think this time it's just a matter of Cash doing what he wants without thought for anyone else. He's not back on drugs, and since he's come here, he's been working and dedicating himself to climbing, not just as a hobby but as a vocation. He's really talented and people think a lot of him."

Pamela sighed. "That's great. But I'm not as optimistic as you seem to be. I've been burned by his behavior too many times before."

Rebecca began to pace. She didn't want to frighten Cash's mother, but maybe she needed to. "This isn't like those other times," she said. "I think something is really wrong. If you have any idea at all—if he mentioned somewhere he intended to go or something he was thinking of doing or hinted at any trouble with anyone—we really need to know about it."

Rebecca's ears rang in the silence that followed. "Pamela?" she asked after a moment. "Are you okay?"

"I'm thinking. And I'm sorry, I don't know anything. Cash knew I didn't approve of his plans, so he didn't talk to me about them."

"If Cash gets in touch with you, will you let me know?" Rebecca asked.

"I will. Though he'd probably call you before he did me. Things haven't been very good between us lately."

"You're still his mother and I know he loves you," Rebecca said. "I'll let you know as soon as I hear anything."

"You do that." Pamela ended the call before Rebecca could say more. She laid the phone on a table and hugged her arms across her chest. Pamela sounded as if she had almost given up on Cash. Rebecca wasn't ready to do that yet. When she saw him again, she was going to give him a big hug—then sit him down for a serious discussion about where his life was headed.

PORTABLE FLOODLIGHTS ringed the old ambulance, the harsh white light glaring off the crime scene techs who combed the area for evidence. The light and flurry of activity made the forest around them seem that much more dark and impenetrable.

County Medical Examiner Dr. Butch Collins, a portly fiftysomething man with short gray hair and deep jowls, emerged from the van and expertly traversed the narrow path marked out by crime scene tape to join Wes and the sheriff on the edge of the clearing. "Your victim is a fit young man who was shot twice, in the side and in the back of the head. Either of those wounds could have killed him," he said.

"I'll know more when I've had time to examine him more closely."

"I only noticed the head wound," Wes said.

"It gets even more interesting," Butch said. "The wound to his side—which could have damaged any number of vital internal organs—had been bandaged some time before he died. I think the head wound occurred later or at least after the victim or someone he was with went to the trouble to bandage the first wound. He wouldn't have been capable of bandaging the first wound after he was shot in the head."

"So it wasn't suicide," the sheriff said.

"Definitely not."

"When did he die?" Wes asked.

"I can't tell you that, either. Not yet," Butch said.

"Do you have any ideas?" Travis asked.

"Rigor has already passed, so more than thirty-six hours. I'll know more after the postmortem."

"Anything else we should know?" Travis asked.

"His hands are pretty battered—busted knuckles and some cuts."

"Did he fight off his killer?" Travis asked.

"I don't think so," Butch said. "The injuries look older than that. From the position of the body, I'd say the second shot was fired after he was already in bed—possibly after he had passed out or even after he was dead."

"He was a rock climber," Wes said. "Maybe the injuries are from that."

Collins nodded. "That's good to know." He looked

back over his shoulder. "We'll transport the body and see what else you find in there."

Sergeant Gage Walker, the sheriff's younger brother, joined them as Collins was leaving. Taller and more outgoing than the sheriff, Gage was the most senior member of the force and Travis's second in command. "As soon as the body is out, you and Wes search the interior," Travis said.

"Ronin shot a ton of photos with the body in place," Gage said. He nodded toward the deputy with a camera. "I'll have him stand by in case we spot anything else we want documented."

Gage turned to Wes. "How did you ever find him? Tucked back in there, that ambulance isn't visible from the road."

"I was told Basher usually kept his camper parked near the climbing area," Wes said. "I came out here looking for him and when I didn't find him there, I drove down the road, thinking he might be pulled over somewhere. I'd given up and was turning around when my headlights glinted off metal and I took a closer look."

"Huh." Gage looked back at the ambulance. "I've seen Basher parked at a couple of different climbing spots around here," he said. "And sometimes behind the guide shop or the Cake Walk Café. I think he worked there as a dishwasher sometimes. It was common knowledge he lived in the old ambulance—I never heard of him even trying to hide the fact. Why were you looking for him?"

"I heard he and Cash Whitlow were friends. I wanted to know if he had seen Cash or knew what was going on with him."

"The interior is free for you to go in." Travis nodded toward the attendants loading a stretcher into a waiting ambulance.

Wes followed Gage up to the ambulance where Deputy Shane Ellis was dusting the door for prints. "Looks like the doors and the whole cab have been wiped," he said as they stopped beside him.

"You can do the rest after Wes and I finish up in the back," Gage commented and stepped up into the vehicle.

"This is a pretty sweet setup," Gage said. He opened a door behind the driver's seat to reveal a toilet and shower. Wire shelves held back accessories and a single towel hung neatly from a hook.

Wes moved past him to the galley area, with a two-burner stove, propane refrigerator and small sink. Cabinets overhead held dishes and dried and canned food, while doors underneath concealed a water tank and on-demand water heater. It was a compact, orderly setup. Wes focused on seeing it, not abstractly but as a window into the inner workings of its occupant. What could this living space tell him about Basher Monroe?

Basher had kept his space orderly and valued his privacy enough to live alone, away from other people, while still clinging to creature comforts like on-demand hot water and indoor plumbing. A rig like this, even if he had done all the work himself, wouldn't have been inexpensive to build, so Basher had gotten the money from somewhere—family or savings, maybe.

Gage emerged from the bathroom. "There's some gauze pads and tape and other first-aid stuff dumped in the sink in there," he said.

"Dr. Collins said he had a bullet wound in his side that had been bandaged," Wes said.

"Better have all the first-aid stuff checked for prints, in case someone else was with him," Gage said. He moved to the built-in dinette. "The wide body of the ambulance gives you a lot of room. And Basher put in a pretty good propane heater. I stopped to check on him after a big storm last winter and it was pretty comfortable in here."

"How long had he been living here?" Wes asked. He opened the refrigerator and studied the contents—some leftover Chinese food, peanut butter, eggs and a few beers.

"I don't know how long he'd been in the ambulance." Gage felt under the cushions on the dinette. "He showed up in Eagle Mountain last summer and stayed. He had Colorado plates, so I always figured he came from somewhere in the area. He told me once that the police in the last place he lived hassled him about living in the ambulance, but as long as he was on public land, or in a private location with permission of the owner, we figured he had as much right to be there as anyone. He never gave us any trouble."

Wes moved to the bed, avoiding looking at the

bloodstained bedding, focusing instead on the night-stand beside the bunk. He picked up the wallet he found there and flipped it open. "His real name was Benjamin," he said. "Benjamin Wade Monroe." He did the math. "He was twenty-eight, and his license gives his address as Bethesda, Maryland." How had Ben become Basher, and how had he gotten from Maryland to Colorado? Was he estranged from his family or simply indulging in an urge to explore and travel? And who had he encountered who wanted him dead?

"Huh." Gage opened the cabinets over the dinette and rifled through the contents.

Wes set the wallet aside. "I'm wondering how the van got back here. Maybe he was afraid of his killer and tried to hide back here."

"Or maybe the killer tucked the ambulance back in here to delay discovery of the body," Gage said.

Wes opened one of two large drawers built under the bunk. Gage moved in beside him and opened the other drawer. "A lot of clothes," Gage said and slid his hand beneath the stacks of T-shirts and shorts.

Wes squatted down and shone his light into the drawer, which extended deep beneath the bunk. Recognition jolted through him, and he reached back and pulled out a bright green shirt.

"Wow, that is ugly," Gage said as Wes spread out the shirt with its pattern of alligators and orange hibiscus flowers against a lime green background.

He reached into the drawer again and pulled out a black wig—the kind of wig you might buy for a

Halloween costume. The kind of wig worn by the man who had come into the guide shop and threatened to kill Cash Whitlow.

BEFORE RETURNING TO work Wednesday morning, Rebecca handed out flyers about Cash at every business she could find open. At the newspaper office, reporter Tammy Patterson promised to write a story about Cash's disappearance, and almost everyone Rebecca talked to told her how much they hoped her nephew was found safe very soon.

Clinic Director Linda Cox welcomed her back warmly. "I saw the flyer about Cash at the coffee shop," she said. "If there's anything we can do to help, let me know."

"Can I post a flyer here?" Rebecca asked.

"Of course."

She had feared she would be too distracted to focus on work, but the clinic was so busy the constant influx of patients and phone calls claimed all her attention. Before she knew it, the whole morning had passed with only fleeting thoughts of Cash.

Linda was preparing to lock the door for lunch when Wes slipped inside. "I just need a word with Rebecca," he said.

Would she ever be able to see him without her heart in her throat? she wondered as she stood to greet him. "We haven't found him yet," he said, anticipating her question. "But I wanted to give you an update before word got out around town. We've found Basher Monroe."

"Does he know where Cash is?" she asked.

"No." His expression was grim. "Basher is dead. He's been murdered."

"Murdered?" She could say the word, but the implication refused to sink in. She swallowed. "That's terrible, but does it have anything to do with Cash?"

"I don't know." He looked toward where two of the medical techs stood, talking. "Could we go somewhere else and talk? It's your lunch break now, right?"

"Yes. I usually eat at my desk."

"Get your lunch and we'll go for a drive. It's probably the only place we can talk without a risk of being overheard."

She retrieved her lunch bag from the refrigerator. "Is everything okay?" Linda asked.

"I think so," Rebecca said. "He just has more questions for me."

She had to wait while he shifted a clipboard, a small duffel and a plastic file box out of the front passenger seat of the black-and-white SUV. "Welcome to my office," he said.

She slid in, trying to avoid contact with the long gun in a holder between the seats and the laptop computer mounted on the dash. A radio squawked and crackled, and he picked up the microphone. "Unit Nine, I'll be 10-7 for the next hour or so."

"10-4, Unit Nine," a woman's voice said.

"I just told dispatch I'm taking a lunch break," he said as he started the vehicle.

"Where are we going?" she asked as he pulled into traffic on Main Street.

"Is the River Park okay? It's a nice day and there usually aren't too many people out there."

"Of course." It felt odd to think of having a discussion about murder and her missing nephew over what amounted to a picnic instead of at the sheriff's office, but the idea wasn't unpleasant.

They didn't speak on the drive to the park, but the silence between them wasn't awkward. She wasn't always comfortable with people she didn't know well, but he was easy to be with. At the park, he retrieved a small cooler from the rear of the vehicle and led the way to a picnic table by the water. "Is this okay?" he asked.

"Sure." The scene was almost too beautiful for a discussion of murder and a missing young man, but it did offer a chance to talk without being overheard.

He sat across from her and took a sandwich and an apple from the cooler, along with a bottle of water. He passed her a second bottle. "Thanks." She unwrapped her own sandwich and stared at it, not sure she could eat. "Tell me about Basher."

"It's not pleasant mealtime conversation," he said. "Don't you want to eat first?"

"Not really." She pushed the sandwich to one side and opened the bottle of water. "How was he killed?"

"He was shot. In his camper in the woods out on

County Road Five. Sometime after he and Cash had lunch together on Sunday."

"Do you know who killed him? Or why?"

Wes shook his head. He took a bite of sandwich, chewed and swallowed before he spoke again. "What can you tell me about Cash's friendship with Basher?"

"Almost nothing," she said. "He might have mentioned they had climbed together a couple of times, but Basher never came by the house and I'm sure I never even spoke to him. Why? Do you think Cash had something to do with his death?" The idea was absurd—and it made her cold with fear.

"We found a wig and a shirt that matched the description of that worn by the man who came into the guide shop yesterday morning and threatened to kill Cash if he didn't do what he was supposed to do," Wes said. "Doug Michelson at the guide shop says he's sure they're what the man was wearing."

"I don't understand," she said. "Why would Basher threaten Cash like that? And why wear a disguise?"

"I was hoping Cash might have said something to you that would help us figure that out," he said.

She shook her head. "It's so…bizarre."

"It is." He took another bite of sandwich. She pinched off a corner of her own sandwich and popped it into her mouth, scarcely tasting it as she chewed.

"That whole scene you described in the guide shop," she said. "The man in the outlandish clothes spouting the clichéd threat—from the beginning I thought it sounded like playacting."

"It sounds that way to me, too," he said. "I'm wondering if someone put Basher up to it. He was known as someone who did odd jobs around town. Maybe someone gave him the wig and shirt and told him what to say."

"And then killed him so he couldn't identify this person?" She shuddered. "Why go to all that trouble?"

"I don't know," he said. "And I'm not sure that scenario fits with the time of death. We're still waiting to hear from the coroner. But I can't help think if we could figure it out, it would help us learn what has happened to Cash."

"What about that shirt I gave you?" she asked. "Have you learned anything about that?"

"Not yet. I sent it to the lab this morning, but it could be several days before we hear back."

"I was afraid you'd say that, but it's hard to be patient at a time like this."

"It's hard for me, too," he said. "And I've had plenty of practice waiting for test results and experts' reports. It never really gets easier."

They continued the meal in silence, the gurgle of the river's current soothing some of her inner turmoil. "A play has to have an audience," she said. "So who was Basher—or whoever was wearing that wig—performing for? Was it meant for Doug?"

"Or for Cash," Wes said. "Maybe the threat was real. Cash did something or said something that made someone upset. Any idea who that might be?"

She shook her head. "No. He hadn't mentioned anything like that."

"What about a drug dealer? When Cash was using, did he ever do favors or odd jobs in exchange for drugs?"

The thought made her feel sick. "I have no idea. He was living in California at the time. But I would swear he wasn't using again. I was always alert for signs and I saw nothing."

"When someone has a history with drugs, it's always something we have to consider," he said.

"Did you find drugs on Basher?" she asked.

"Only a little marijuana—nothing illegal."

She folded the wrapper around her mostly uneaten sandwich and shoved it back into her lunch bag. "I hate not being able to do more to help," she said. "I've handed out posters, and I keep calling and texting Cash's number, hoping he'll answer. But it doesn't seem to be doing any good."

"I thought I'd go this evening and talk to some more climbers," Wes said. "Doug told me some areas they like to gather in the late afternoon to climb and trade tips. Would you like to come with me?"

"Do you think that would help?" she asked.

"I do. They might be more willing to talk to you than to me."

"Of course. I'll do anything to help."

"They're going to do the aerial search this afternoon and you did a good job of distributing flyers around town. Maybe someone will have some information for us soon."

"The longer he remains missing, the further away he feels," she said. She stared out toward the rippling water. "I called Cash's mom, Pamela, last night after you left my place. I'd been putting off talking to her, hoping to have good news, but I couldn't wait any longer."

"What did she have to say?" he asked.

How to describe her sister-in-law's reaction? "Pamela has had a hard time with Cash these last few years. She had to deal with him dropping out of school, his drug addiction and his wanting to pursue climbing, even though that's what killed his father. I think at this point she's expended so much emotional energy she doesn't have anything left to give."

"What did she say when you told her Cash was missing?"

"She said she hopes he's okay and that we find him soon, but I should remember that he has always been very insistent on making his own decisions, and has never been willing to take advice from others. If he's made another bad decision this time, I shouldn't feel guilty about it." She stared down at her fists, clenched on the picnic table in front of her. "That probably sounds cold, but she isn't like that. She's just been hurt so many times, by Scott's death, then by things Cash has done. I think that attempt at distance is her way of coping."

"Do you think it's possible Cash decided to go back

to California and didn't tell you because he thought you'd be disappointed?"

"No. Cash wasn't the type to worry about disappointing other people. I don't mean that as a criticism. He was like Scott that way—when he made up his mind about something, he didn't care what other people thought about the decision. He did what he thought was right for him. That could be frustrating at times, especially when his decisions—like quitting school—seemed unwise. But part of me admired that he was so confident of his own judgment."

"He sounds like a very interesting young man. I'm looking forward to meeting him."

She looked up and his gaze caught and held hers. She might have kissed him at that moment, she was so grateful that he still talked as if finding Cash alive and well was only a matter of time.

Chapter Five

Dr. Butch Collins suggested Wes and Travis stop by his office Wednesday afternoon. "I'm going to put everything I have to tell you in my report, but I know you're going to have questions," he said. "So you might as well save us all the delay and stop by."

Collins's office very much reflected the man, with fishing gear and hunting trophies sharing space with his medical license and commendations. He stood from behind a large, cluttered desk to greet them, then invited them to sit and shuffled through the stacks of paper on his desk until he found what he wanted. He passed a folder across to Travis. "There's the report, but the upshot is, Basher Monroe was shot at two different times, by two different weapons—a 45 caliber and a 12-gauge shotgun slug." He passed over two labeled evidence bags. "The slug is the one that killed him. The wound didn't look like much from the outside, but it caused massive internal injuries."

"So he was shot by two different people?" Wes asked.

"It gets even more interesting," Butch said. "The second shot—the one in his head—was made after he was dead. He was in bed, so the killer may not have known he was dead, and thought he was sleeping. Shot him in the head and left."

"It could have been the same person who shot him earlier, come back to finish the job," Travis said.

"But he brings a different gun this time?" Wes asked.

"How long had he been dead when he was shot?" Travis asked.

"I can't be certain, but enough time had passed for Basher, or someone else, to have bandaged the first wound and Basher to have gone to bed, where he died, probably after several hours of suffering. If he had sought medical treatment immediately after he was shot, he might have survived, but he might not have. In any case, by the time the second shooter showed up, Basher's heart had stopped beating and his blood had stopped circulating."

"Is there anything significant about the bandage?" Wes asked.

Butch nodded. "An amateur job, clumsily tied, but it would have been awkward doing it himself."

"Do you think he had help?" Travis asked.

"Probably, though I can't be absolutely sure."

"Do you have an estimate on the time of death?" Wes asked.

"I'd say between noon and four on Monday," Butch said. "He was a strong man. Considering the nature of the wound, he took a long time to die."

"And you're sure he died in bed?"

"Yes."

"Anything else we need to know?" Travis asked.

"Everything I found is in my report, but nothing significant beyond what I've already told you."

Travis stood and tapped the edge of the file on the desk. "Thanks, Butch," he said.

"I'll be interested to know how this one turns out," Butch said.

"I'll be interested to know how this turns out, too," Wes said as he and Travis walked toward the sheriff's SUV.

"The preliminary forensics on the crime scene came in this morning," Travis said. "There's no indication that the killer searched the ambulance or stole anything from it, though we can't be positive about that. Maybe he stole something small and was very neat about his search. We've hauled the ambulance to our impound lot for a more thorough search, but we didn't discover any fingerprints, except Basher's on the inside of a couple of cabinets. Everything else had been wiped down. No shoe impressions or tire impressions at the scene."

"So the killer had enough time to clean up after himself," Wes said. "That's a pretty remote area, so he must have driven there. Maybe someone in the area saw his vehicle."

"There aren't any houses nearby," Travis said. "But one of the climbers leaving the area might have passed the killer. It's worth asking about."

"A man wearing a black wig and a tropical print shirt like the one we found among Basher's belongings was at Colorado Mountain Guides just after two o'clock on Monday," Wes said. "It couldn't have been Basher. He was either dead or very near death at that time."

"So, was the man who came to the guide shop looking for Cash the same man who killed Basher?" Travis asked. "Or the person who shot Basher the second time? Maybe he came to the ambulance looking for Basher, saw him in bed and thought he was sleeping, shot him, then stashed the wig and shirt in with Basher's things."

"I've asked the lab to check for DNA and hair on the clothing and wig," Wes said. "Maybe they'll find something. I'm also going to press the lab about the analysis of the bloodstain on Cash Whitlow's shirt. I'm wondering now if it's a match for Basher. I know he and Cash were together on Sunday. The manager of Mo's Tavern, George Christopher, says the two of them had lunch together there and were involved in what he described as a serious conversation. They left together in Cash's Toyota pickup. I haven't been able to track their whereabouts for the rest of the day, until about six-thirty, when Cash returned to his aunt's house. He left after supper and came back again about midnight, then left sometime after Rebecca went to work Monday morning at eight and hasn't been seen since. We have one report of the ambulance Basher had converted to a camper being parked in the parking area for a climbing area known as the Falls, off

County Road Five, approximately one and a half miles from where we found the ambulance on Monday afternoon."

Travis nodded, but made no comment. Wes kept reviewing everything he knew about Basher and Cash. Had the two friends fallen out and Cash shot Basher? Then who was the other shooter who had fired the bullet into Basher's head? Was the blood on Cash's shirt from Basher or someone else? Rebecca hadn't mentioned Cash being hurt, but could he have hidden that fact from his aunt? Could the blood be his own?

Deputy Jamie Douglas met them in the hallway of the sheriff's department. "I spoke with Mary Ann Schwartz just before I came on shift," she said. "She told me she and a friend went out to the Falls about eight o'clock Monday morning and Basher's ambulance wasn't there. Mary Ann works at Eagle Mountain Grocery and she volunteered this information when I dropped Donna at work this morning. She said Basher's rig was parked near the Falls when she drove out there Sunday afternoon to meet a friend, and he usually stays parked at one spot for weeks, so she was a little surprised to see he wasn't there Monday."

Donna was Jamie's younger sister, Wes recalled. He was still putting together all the relationships between his coworkers. Jamie was married to an officer with Colorado Parks and Wildlife, and Donna, who had Down syndrome, lived with them.

"Thanks," Wes said. "So Basher or someone else

moved the ambulance sometime between Sunday afternoon and Monday evening when I located it."

"So what's the link between Basher and Cash?" Jamie asked. "Could they have had an argument that got out of hand, Cash shot Basher, then freaked out and ran? Or did the same person who shot Basher go after Cash and he fled? Or he's dead, too, and we just haven't found him yet?"

"We haven't found Cash's truck or any clue as to where he might be," Wes said.

"There are a lot of canyons and gorges and old mines where a truck or a person would be easy to hide," Jamie said. "Or maybe Rebecca's first supposition is right, and Cash went climbing by himself, somewhere off the beaten track, had an accident and was unable to call for help. If that's the case, it will take more luck than skill to find him."

"Delta Farm Spray did an aerial search for us this morning with one of their helicopters," Travis said. "They focused on canyons, cliffs and peaks that might be attractive to a climber, but they didn't find anything."

"We're not getting much out of the climbing community," Wes said. "When I speak to them, they say a lot of general stuff about what a talented climber Cash was, but they all say they don't know anything about his personal life."

"Maybe we need to lean on them a little more to get at the truth," Travis said.

"I plan to go back out to Caspar Canyon this evening," Wes said. "A lot of climbers gather there after they get off work. I thought I'd take Rebecca Whitlow with me. A lot of them know her and if she asked for their help, maybe they'd be a little more forthcoming."

"We're talking about two active young men with lots of friends," Travis said. "Someone knows something about what happened."

"I THOUGHT WE'D try Caspar Canyon first," Wes said when he picked up Rebecca at her house that evening. She had changed from her work clothes into jeans and a light sweater, but he was still in his khaki uniform. "Are you familiar with the area?"

"Oh, yes. I've spent a lot of hours watching my brother, and then Cash, train and compete there and other climbing spots around here."

"Did you ever do any climbing yourself?" Wes asked.

"Some. But I never competed. I didn't enjoy it the way Scott and his friends did. Actually, I'm a little afraid of heights. I'm more comfortable cheering from ground level."

"I'm with you there," he said. He headed toward the highway leading out of town. "I'm going to let you do most of the talking today. Sometimes my uniform and badge get in the way of people telling the whole story. I'm hoping they'll be more forthcoming with you."

"All right. But what do I say? Do I just ask if they've seen Cash or know where he planned on going?"

"Those are good places to start, but there are some

things I need you to try to find out." He glanced at her. "I know it makes you uncomfortable, but I need you to ask about drugs."

"But—"

"I know you don't believe Cash was involved with drugs," he interrupted. "And you may be right. But maybe his friend Basher was. Or maybe someone else was trying to get him back into that life. We need to know."

"All right."

"Ask if anyone had threatened Cash or if he was afraid of anyone."

Every possibility he raised seemed worse than the last, but if she was going to help, she had to face that. "I hate to think something like that was going on with him and I didn't realize it," she said.

"Don't beat yourself up," he said. "We're talking about a nineteen-year-old guy. They're not into sharing feelings much, especially with an aunt."

The comment surprised a laugh from her. "I guess you're right about that."

He signaled the turn onto the Forest Service road that led into a deep, narrow canyon that was popular with rock climbers in the summer and ice climbers in the winter. The rugged canyon walls offered everything from basic beginning routes to more challenging climbs. A dirt pull-off marked the start of the most popular section of wall, and Wes turned into this and parked. Half a dozen climbers were arranged on the cliff or on the ground. Several of them turned to look as Wes pulled the black-and-white SUV into the parking area. "See anyone you know?" he asked.

"Dave Hammersmith—everyone calls him Hammer—is in the blue climbing helmet with the young woman I don't know," she said. "Garth is the man with him—I don't know his last name. And I think that's Sam Mason on the cliff on the far left. He and Cash competed in several competitions I attended."

"Good. Start with the folks you know. Take one of the flyers and start with that."

They got out of the SUV and she walked toward the trio of two young men and a woman on the ground at the base of the cliffs. They watched, stone-faced, as she and Wes drew near. "Hey, Hammer," she said, addressing the shorter red-haired young man in the blue climbing helmet.

He nodded. "Hi, Rebecca." His gaze flicked to Wes, then back to her.

"I'm trying to get out as many of these flyers as I can," she said. "Spread the word about Cash."

Hammer took the flyer and looked at it. "I saw one of these at the coffee shop in town," he said. "I was sorry to hear about Cash."

"I'm really worried he went climbing somewhere on his own and is hurt." She looked at each of them. "Did any of you ever hear him mention any area—maybe a new route or something—that he wanted to climb?"

All three shook their heads. "I've been looking for

him," the young woman said. "Hammer and I even drove around some this morning, looking for his truck."

"Kaitlyn and I drove miles," Hammer said. "I'm sorry we couldn't find him. We checked everywhere we could think of."

"When was the last time you saw him?" Rebecca asked, addressing the question to all three.

"We climbed with him on Saturday," Kaitlyn said. "He was having a great day, climbing this really gnarly ridge like it was nothing. We were talking about going up to Grand Teton at the end of the summer to climb and we told him he should join us. He said he'd like that, though he was hoping to find a youth camp or something that would hire him for the season."

Garth turned and addressed Wes. "Is it true somebody killed Basher?"

"Yes," Wes said. "Do you know anyone who might have wanted him dead?"

"No," Garth said. "What happened?"

"We found him in his ambulance. Someone shot him."

Garth swore. "Do you know who did it?"

"No. Had he argued with anyone? Did he ever talk about someone being after him?"

"Not Basher," Hammer said. "The guy was super mellow. All he cared about was climbing and traveling around in that ambulance. It was a sweet life. I can't believe someone would have it in for him."

"I was wondering if maybe Basher was into drugs," Rebecca said.

"No way," Garth said. "I mean, a little pot or beer, but that's not illegal." He cut his eyes to Wes.

"You know, Cash struggled with addiction in the past," Rebecca said. "I worried he might fall back into that."

"He didn't," Garth said.

"How can you be so sure?" Wes asked.

"Because he was so focused on staying healthy," Garth said. "He was determined to be the best climber ever and for that, you have to be in top shape."

"Cash didn't even drink beer," Kaitlyn said. "He wouldn't smoke anything, either. Some of the guys gave him a hard time about it."

"Not me," Hammer said. "I thought it just showed how dedicated he was."

"Did you ever hear anyone threaten Cash or Basher?" Wes asked. "Maybe they were trespassing on private land or someone was jealous of their skills?"

All three shook their heads. "That stuff happens, yeah," Garth said. "But I never heard it happening to either of them."

Rebecca pressed several flyers into his hand. "Could you pass these out to anyone you think could help?" she asked. "And tell them to give me a call if they know anything. Even if you think it's not important, it could help."

"Sure. And I hope you find him soon and he's okay." He turned to Wes. "I hope you find who killed

Basher. He was kind of an odd guy, but he never hurt anyone."

Rebecca and Wes moved on to the climbers up on the wall. One by one, as each descended, Rebecca handed him or her a flyer and asked about Cash. But none of them had seen or talked to him recently or knew anything about his plans. When there was no one left to talk to, they returned to the SUV.

She settled into the passenger seat and sighed. She had hoped speaking with Cash's friends would bring them closer to finding him, but she only felt more confused.

"Thanks for coming with me to talk to the climbers," Wes said.

"Do you really think it did any good?"

"We got a little information we didn't have before. I know some new questions to ask."

"We keep asking all these questions," she said. "I'm ready for some answers." And soon. Before Cash's time ran out.

Chapter Six

"The climbers we spoke with yesterday were adamant that neither Cash nor Basher were involved with drugs, and they couldn't think of anyone who would want to harm either of them," Wes reported at the Thursday morning meeting at the sheriff's department.

"No mention of Cash wanting to leave town or having a disagreement with his aunt that might have led to him deciding to move on?" Gage asked.

"Nothing like that." He checked the notes he'd made right after their conversation with the climbers. "He talked about getting a job this summer working with kids, maybe at a youth camp."

"Trey Allerton is supposedly building some kind of youth camp on the land he leased from Sam Russell," Shane said.

"But there isn't actually a camp yet, right?" Wes asked. He had helped with the investigation of rancher Sam Russell's murder, and had visited the ranch. Trey Allerton had been questioned in that case, and in the murder of a young woman by Allerton's former business partner, but Wes hadn't personally met the man.

"Allerton has been busy talking up the project and raising a lot of money, but he hasn't done much when it comes to actual construction of his youth ranch," Shane said. "I can't see that he'd be in a position to hire employees yet."

"Go talk to Allerton," Travis said. "Jamie, you go with him." The sheriff slid back his chair and stood. "Allerton thinks he's charming. If you pretend to be impressed, he might let down his guard. He may not know anything about Cash, but I'm curious to find out if they crossed paths."

"I know the type." Jamie stood also. "I'll do my best." She turned to Wes. "Have you been to Allerton's place before?"

He shook his head. "Only to the main ranch."

"Then I'll drive. Prepare to be unimpressed."

On the way to Allerton's place, Jamie filled Wes in on what she knew about Trey Allerton. "He was in the army with Shane's fiancée's brother," she said. "That's how Shane and Lauren met—she came to us because her brother's widow went missing in this area. Or rather, she'd run off with Allerton and broke contact with everyone else. Allerton claimed to be the brother's best friend and apparently romanced the widow after the brother was killed in action. He sold her on the idea of building this youth ranch and apparently she's footing the bill for most of it from money she inherited.

"But he seems to keep associating with murderers," Wes said. In addition to his former business partner who killed a local woman, a man Allerton hired to work for him murdered Sam Russell.

"He's either incredibly unlucky when it comes to picking associates, or he's attracted to a criminal element," Jamie said. "I'll let you make your own judgment when you meet him. I'm interested in what you make of him."

Allerton's residence, as Jamie had warned, was unimpressive. The metal-sided mobile home had been painted turquoise at some point in the past, though the color had softened to a dusty pastel. The area in front of the trailer was dirt, and no attempt had been made to landscape the sagebrush and weeds that passed for a yard. "How many acres does he have?" Wes asked as he and Jamie climbed out of her cruiser.

"Sixty acres. He says there's going to be bunkhouses and cabins for the kids and staff, a stable and hiking trails, a dining hall and who knows what else."

Wes looked around at the expanse of sagebrush and cactus, a leaning barbed wire fence stretching toward the horizon. "How long has he been here?" he asked.

"Three months," Jamie said.

"Not that much time when you consider the scope of the project he's proposing," Wes said.

"Maybe not," Jamie said. She led the way to the set of wooden steps that led to the front door of the trailer, and knocked.

"Who is it?" a woman's voice called through the door.

"Deputy Jamie Douglas and Deputy Wes Landry, from the Rayford County Sheriff's Department. Is that you, Ms. Baker?"

"Trey isn't here," the woman said. "I don't know when he'll be back."

Jamie's eyes met Wes's, worry tightening her expression. "Could you open the door so we can talk to you a few minutes, Ms. Baker?" she asked.

A chain rattled and a lock turned, then the door eased open.

Courtney Baker was a petite blonde who might have been any age from twenty-five to forty. Though her features hinted at beauty, her long hair hung limp, obscuring half her face, and her T-shirt and jeans sagged on her slight frame. "Ms. Baker, are you all right?" Jamie asked. "Have you been ill?"

"I'm fine." Courtney squared her shoulders. "What do you want? I told you, Trey isn't here."

"Where is he?" Jamie tried to look past her. "And where is your daughter, Ashlyn?"

The lines around Courtney's mouth deepened. "Ashlyn is with Trey. He likes to take her with him when he's working."

"Can we come in?" Wes asked.

"Now isn't a good time." Courtney started to close the door but Wes shot out a hand to stop her.

"Wait." He held out one of Rebecca's flyers. "Have you seen this young man? He's missing and his family is very worried about him."

Courtney took the flyer and studied it for a long

moment, though the fall of hair in front of her face hid her expression. At last she handed it back to Wes. "I'm sorry, I haven't seen him."

"We were wondering if Trey had talked to him about his youth ranch," he said. "Cash mentioned wanting to work with kids."

"No," she said. "I'm sorry, I can't help you." This time she succeeded in closing the door, and they heard the lock click into place.

"Something is really wrong," Jamie said when they were back in the cruiser.

"She wasn't very happy to see us," Wes said. "Do you think she's lying about having seen Cash?"

"I don't know about that, but everything about her is wrong. She's lost weight since I saw her last and she looks terrible." She stared toward the trailer. "When I first met her, she was this gorgeous, perfectly put-together woman—hair curled, nails done, clothes just so. And you saw her now. Everything about her is different."

"Maybe we caught her on a bad day," Wes said. "She wasn't expecting company."

"Did you see how she kept her hair all down in front of her face? I think she was hiding something."

"Such as?"

"I think she had a black eye. I couldn't be sure, but I thought I glimpsed bruising." Jamie gripped the steering wheel. "I have half a mind to go back up there and confront her."

"You could try," Wes said. "But I don't think it will

do any good. She had plenty of opportunities to ask us for help and she didn't."

"It bothers me that Allerton has her little girl, too." Jamie shuddered. "Maybe Courtney didn't say anything because Allerton threatened to hurt Ashlyn."

"Do you think he'd do that?" Wes asked.

"I don't know," she said. "He comes across as a charming, all-American guy who just wants to help kids, but to me that always felt like an act. Like underneath the mask he's much darker."

"We could sit here and wait for Allerton and Ashlyn to return," Wes said.

"Not here." She started the cruiser's engine. "We'll park up the road a ways, where he can't see us. If he's up to something, I'd like nothing better than to catch him in the act."

REBECCA WAS WORKING the clinic's reception desk on Thursday afternoon when a handsome blond man approached, a little girl in tow. "May I help you?" she asked.

"We don't have an appointment or anything. I just need to check my stepdaughter's vaccination records," he said. "Her mom couldn't remember if they're up-to-date."

Rebecca leaned forward to smile at the little girl, a blue-eyed blonde who shyly returned the smile. "What's your name, honey?" she asked.

"Ashlyn Baker," the man said before the girl could answer and offered her date of birth."

Rebecca typed in the information and pulled up the girl's record. Under parents' names, only her mother, Courtney Baker, was listed. "What is your name, sir?" she asked.

"I'm Trey Allerton." He grinned, a dimple forming on the left side of his mouth and the fine lines deepening around his blue eyes.

"And you are Ashlyn's stepfather?" Rebecca asked.

He leaned closer and lowered his voice. "Her mother and I aren't actually married, but since her father passed away several years ago, I'm definitely the father figure in her life."

"I'm sorry, but I can only give out medical information to an authorized person," Rebecca said. "If Ashlyn's mother will stop by, I can give her Ashlyn's vaccination records."

"I understand. I just thought I'd check as long as we were in town."

She nodded and expected him to move away. Instead, he struck a casual pose, leaning against the pillar beside the front counter. "Aren't you Rebecca Whitlow?" he asked.

"Yes."

"I saw the flyers about your nephew, Cash. I'm really sorry to hear he's missing."

"Thank you. Do you know Cash? Have you seen him recently?"

Allerton shook his head. "No, I just know of him. I saw the article in the local paper. He sounds like quite an accomplished young man."

"He is. If you see him or his truck or know anything about him, we'd appreciate it if you'd call one of the numbers on the flyer."

"Oh, I will. It's really amazing in a town this small no one has seen or heard anything."

She nodded and focused on the computer. This man's interest was beginning to bother her. Was this his idea of flirting?

"Did Cash know that young man who was murdered?" Allerton asked. "I heard he was a climber, too."

This was starting to feel creepy. "I really don't have time to talk," she said. "I have work to do."

He straightened. "Sure. I didn't mean to bother you."

The door from the back of the office opened and physician's assistant Lauren Baker entered. "Trey, what are you doing here?" she asked.

"Aunt Lauren!" Ashlyn stood on tiptoe to see over the counter and grinned at her aunt.

Lauren returned the smile. "Hey, Ashlyn." She hurried across the office and through the door leading to the waiting room. The little girl ran and threw her arms around her. Lauren gathered Ashlyn into her arms and turned to Trey. "Where's Courtney?" she asked.

"She's back at the ranch. Ashlyn and I are having an afternoon out together." He smiled at the little girl, but Lauren put a protective arm around her and took a step back.

Allerton held out his hand. "Come on, Ashlyn," he said. "We need to go."

"I want to stay with Aunt Lauren." The little girl tightened her hold around Lauren's neck.

"Aunt Lauren has work today," Allerton said. "Come on. I'll buy you an ice cream."

"You don't have to go with him if you don't want," Lauren said.

"I want ice cream." Ashlyn pushed out of Lauren's arms and hurried to join Trey.

He took the child's hand and gave Lauren a smug look.

"Tell Courtney to call me," Lauren said as he headed for the door.

He said nothing, merely left. Lauren hurried back into the office. "What did he want?" she asked Rebecca.

"He asked about Ashlyn's vaccination records. He said he was her stepfather."

"He is most definitely not her stepfather." Lauren's voice was brittle. "I hope you didn't tell him anything."

"Of course not. He isn't listed on her records as authorized to receive any information."

"Sorry. I wasn't implying you don't know your job. Trey Allerton just makes me so angry."

"He's your sister's boyfriend?" Rebecca asked.

"Sister-in-law. Courtney is my brother's widow. Trey Allerton was in the army with my brother, Mike, though I never heard him mention the man. He showed up one day and poured on the charm and Courtney fell for it. Now he has her living in a trailer on some ranch land he leased, financing his dream of building a camp for troubled youth—though so far no one has seen evidence that he's doing anything more than fundraising at this point. I can't believe Courtney let him take Ashlyn off alone. I wouldn't trust him with my pet cat—and she has claws to defend herself."

"Ashlyn didn't seem upset about being with him," Rebecca said carefully.

"Ashlyn is barely three years old," Lauren said. She shook her head. "Why would Trey need to know about her vaccination records?"

"I'm not sure if that wasn't just an excuse to talk to me," Rebecca said. When Lauren stared at her, she flushed. "He was asking a lot of questions about Cash, and about Basher Monroe."

"You need to tell the sheriff," Lauren said.

"Why?" The idea alarmed Rebecca.

"Trey Allerton has a history with them. Two people he associated with were murderers. If he was asking about Basher, maybe it's because he knows something."

Gail, one of the techs, stuck her head into the office. "Lauren? Dr. Mezaluna is on line three," she said.

Lauren left and, after she checked that no one was waiting for her, Rebecca dialed Wes's number. The call went to voice mail. She left a message for him to call her, then tried to focus on the billing information she needed to enter into the computer. The visit from

Trey Allerton had been upsetting, though she couldn't articulate why. He was probably one of those people who got a thrill out of being close to tragedy, as long as it wasn't their own.

JAMIE MANEUVERED THE cruiser behind a stand of pinion trees alongside the road, a few hundred yards and slightly uphill from Trey Allerton's driveway. "We'll be able to see Trey when he gets home," she said. "He drives a black F-150." She lowered the windows before switching off the engine.

Quiet enveloped them. A warm breeze carried the scents of dirt and sagebrush. "Not much traffic up here," he said.

"There are some hiking trails near an abandoned mine at the far end of the road," Jamie said. "But they don't get a lot of use. A young couple live in a yurt about a mile farther on, and there's an old guy who lives on some mining claims past them, and that's about it."

"What's the guy mining?" Wes asked. "Gold? Silver?"

"I don't know," Jamie said. "Supposedly there's still some of each around here, plus a lot of rare earth minerals—the stuff they use to make cell phones and computers. But there must not be enough to make it worth putting in all the effort to get to it. I think Martin Kramer is just one of those eccentric people who march to a different drummer. He's kind of a grouch, really, but he isn't hurting anyone."

"I guess it's not a bad life, if you like your own company," he said. He had never aspired to be a hermit, but there were times when he saw the beauty of being alone.

"How do you like Eagle Mountain?" Jamie asked.

"I like it," he said. "I enjoy the outdoors, and the slower pace."

"I imagine it's a lot slower than St. Louis," she said.

Slow was exactly what he had been hoping for when he moved here. Or rather a more reasonable pace, with time to devote to each case and enough hours off to recuperate. "I'm not bored," he said. "I like the variety of the work and I'm enjoying getting to know the area."

"I like that about this job, too," she said. "What did you do with the St. Louis police?"

He didn't really want to talk about this, but he supposed the questions were only natural. "I worked Vice my last four years there," he said.

She wrinkled her nose. "I get that it's really important work, but I'm not sure I could stand always dealing with the worst side of people. Still, it must have been pretty satisfying to put some of those criminals away."

He shifted in his seat. "It was." And very frustrating when some of them managed to escape justice time after time. "What more can you tell me about Trey Allerton?" he asked.

She shrugged. "You probably already know everything I know. He's leasing this land from the Russell

Ranch and is raising money to build a camp where troubled or disadvantaged youth can spend time in the outdoors. I gather Courtney is financing most of it, though Trey has mentioned *investors* without naming names. He can be very charming, so maybe he has raised a lot of money, though as you can see, no signs of construction yet."

"What do you know about Courtney Baker?" Wes asked.

"Shane is the one to ask about her," Jamie said. "His fiancé, Lauren, is Courtney's sister-in-law. Her late husband was Lauren's brother. She apparently inherited a lot of money and was living a comfortable life in Denver and left it all to live in that junky trailer out here in the middle of nowhere."

"Maybe she wanted a complete change," Wes said. He could relate to that, though he hadn't opted for quite so rustic an existence.

"And maybe Trey Allerton is a really great partner and intends to go through with his plans for his youth camp, and I'm just overly suspicious," Jamie said. "But something about him doesn't feel right to me."

"Cop sense," Wes said. After so much time on the job, some people developed a sixth sense about crime.

"I guess." She ran her palms along the steering wheel. "Do you feel that way about people or situations sometimes?"

"Sometimes," he said. "But I haven't always been right." Being wrong about those intuitions could be disastrous.

The staccato blast of distant gunfire made them both sit up straighter.

"It's not hunting season," Jamie said.

"Maybe someone target shooting," Wes said.

Another burst of gunfire. Jamie started the cruiser. "Maybe we'd better check it out."

"Yeah." He reminded himself he wasn't in the city anymore. Rural people might be shooting at a predator or sighting in a hunting rifle.

But he wouldn't soon forget the sight of Basher Monroe shot in his bed. Murder happened even in peaceful places like this, as much as he wished it weren't so.

Chapter Seven

Jamie turned in at the first driveway on the left, and bumped the cruiser to a halt in front of a green-sided yurt. As she and Wes waited, listening for more gunfire, a young man in brown cargo shorts and a faded black T-shirt came around the side of the yurt and moved toward them at a leisurely pace.

Jamie rolled down her window. "Hey, Robby," she called. "We thought we heard gunshots."

Robby, a man in his twenties with short reddish hair, stopped beside the driver's side window. "That was probably just Mr. Kramer," he said.

"What's he shooting at?" Wes asked.

"Probably nothing." Robby leaned down and looked across at Wes. "Mr. Kramer is kind of an eccentric old guy. He's paranoid about someone trying to steal his gold. We've learned if we go up there, we need to stop away from the house and honk the horn to let him know it's us."

"Does he have a lot of gold?" Jamie asked.

Robby shrugged. "Who knows? We've heard rumors that he does, but I suspect those may have been started by him. Anyway, he has a tendency to shoot at anything that moves. He's convinced they're coming for his gold. I don't know if there's some real mental illness, or dementia, or what's going on, but Becca and I try to keep an eye on him. We check on him at least once a week and Becca bakes for him, or we take him produce from our greenhouse. When he's not ranting about people trying to steal from him, he's really an interesting guy. He used to be an engineer in Ohio, and he's traveled all over the world."

"He's lucky to have you two for neighbors," Jamie said. "What about the folks in the trailer down the road?" She nodded toward Allerton's place. "Do you see much of them?"

"Nothing," Robby said. "We went down there to introduce ourselves and take them some fresh produce and the man told us they preferred to keep to themselves and didn't like unannounced visitors. He wasn't mean about it or anything, just very straightforward—*we're busy and don't have time to socialize.* I guess that's their right. We still wave when we pass one of them on the road, but they don't wave back."

"That's an odd way to behave," Jamie said.

"Yeah, well, some people really do move off-grid because they want to be completely alone."

Wes took out one of the flyers about Cash Whitlow and passed it over to Robby. "Have you seen this young man around?" he asked.

Robby studied the flyer and shook his head. "I haven't. Do you think he was climbing around here?"

"We don't know," Wes said. "Do people climb near here?"

"I don't think so," Robby said. "But I don't know much about the sport."

He tried to hand back the flyer but Wes waved him off. "Keep it. Show it to your wife. Maybe she's seen him or his truck."

"I don't think so, but I'll show it to her."

"I think we'll drive up to the Full Moon Mine and make sure everything is all right," Jamie said.

"Be careful," Robby said. "I don't think Mr. Kramer likes law enforcement any more than he does anyone else."

Robby watched as Jamie turned the cruiser and headed out the drive again. "Those two didn't exactly hit the jackpot with their neighbors," Wes said.

"I'm surprised Courtney Baker would be so standoffish," Jamie said. "Lauren described her as very friendly and outgoing, and you'd think she would welcome company up here so far from town."

She slowed as the cruiser climbed a hill, then rounded a curve, and stopped at a sign that read Full Moon Mine. No Trespassing. Owner is Armed. "This is the place," she said and turned into a narrow rutted drive.

When they were in sight of a cabin, she stopped and tapped her horn. A few second later, a figure emerged from the cabin, and she inched the cruiser forward.

Up close, the cabin was more of a shack, constructed of rough-hewn logs, stood on end, the bark peeling off in long strips. The man who stood in front of the structure had a gray beard, but an erect posture, and wore dirty canvas trousers and a faded plaid shirt.

Jamie stopped the vehicle and rolled down the window. "Good afternoon, Mr. Kramer," she said.

"What do you want?" Kramer barked.

"We heard gunshots," she said. "Is everything all right?"

Kramer stalked toward them. "A man's got a right to protect himself and his property," he said.

"What happened?" Jamie asked. "Why were you shooting?"

"I was shooting at a two-legged varmint who's been trying to rob me blind," he said. He bent low and looked in at Wes. "I don't recognize you. Who are you?"

"I'm Deputy Wes Landry. Who is this person who's trying to rob you?"

"If I knew that, I'd march down to the sheriff's office and file charges," Kramer said. "But he's a sneaky devil. He comes around at night or when I'm working in the mine."

"And he was here just now?" Wes asked.

"Maybe. I thought I heard something. The other night was a full moon and I got a good look at him."

"What does he look like?" Wes asked.

"He was young. Young enough to be fast. He was wearing one of those sweatshirt things with a hood, the hood pulled up so I couldn't see his face, and jeans."

"What night was this?" Wes asked.

"Monday. After midnight. I got an alarm set up in the mine so I can hear when anyone but me goes in there and it went off. This wasn't the first time he was in there, just the first time I got a look at him."

"And you shot at him?" Jamie asked.

"I did. He ran away. And he'd better not come back. Next time I might not miss."

"Next time, call us instead of trying to take matters into your own hands," Wes said.

"Phones don't work up here, or didn't you know that?" Kramer said. "By the time I got to where I could call you people and got back here, the thieves would have robbed me blind."

"Do you think more than one person is involved?" Wes asked.

"Maybe." Kramer stuck out his lip in a caricature of stubbornness.

"What have they stolen from you?" Jamie asked.

"They took a bucket of ore samples and an old copper kettle I use for heating water. They broke the lock on my cabin door and rummaged around, but they didn't find where I hide the real valuables. But they keep coming back to try again."

"How many times have they been here?" Jamie asked.

"Two or three. Four, if that was them I heard today."

"How do they get here?" Wes asked. "Do they come in a car or truck?"

"I don't care if they come in a spaceship, they're trespassing," Kramer said.

Wes took a steadying breath. Questioning Kramer was like trying to pin down quicksilver. "If you had a vehicle description, it might help us find these people," he said.

"Well I don't," he said. "And I don't have time to wait around for you people to solve my problems. I can take care of myself."

"Mr. Kramer, please don't do anything rash," Jamie said.

"I know what you think," he said. "You think I'm a senile old man who's seeing things that aren't there. But I'm not a fool. These are real people and I've got real bullets in my gun that will take care of the problem sooner or later."

"What kind of ammo are you shooting?" Wes asked.

"Bird shot. Not that it's any of your business." He took a step back. "Now get out of here and leave me alone."

Wes sensed that Jamie wanted to argue, but she pressed her lips together and shifted into Reverse. Neither of them said anything until they were on the Forest Service road again. "Do you think someone is really stealing from him?" she asked.

"I don't know," Wes said.

"We should have asked to see the broken door lock," she said.

"He would have probably said he already fixed it."

"So you think he's lying?"

"Not lying. But maybe exaggerating. Or misinterpreting what's going on."

"As bad as it is to think of him terrified of figments of his imagination, I hope real people aren't involved," Jamie said. "If he doesn't kill someone shooting at them, they're liable to hurt him shooting back."

"I'd like to know if he always shoots bird shot or if he uses slugs, too," Wes said.

"You're thinking of Basher Monroe," Jamie said. "But lots of people have shotguns."

"Yes, but Kramer has a reputation for using his."

"The camper where Basher died is a long way from here," Jamie said. "From the description of his wounds in the autopsy report, I don't see how Basher could have been shot at Kramer's place and gotten back to that ambulance before he was dead."

"Basher was a young strong guy, who maybe didn't realize he'd been hurt as badly as he was," Wes said. "And if he had someone to help him get back to his ambulance…"

"Someone like Cash Whitlow." Jamie nodded. "It's something to think about."

"In the meantime, we'll report this to the sheriff," Wes said. "He may want to add some extra patrols up this way."

Jamie slowed as they neared Allerton's trailer. A

black Ford pickup sat in the driveway now. She turned in and parked behind the truck. "Let's see what Allerton has to say for himself," she said.

Wes knocked on the door this time, but no answer and no sounds from within the trailer. He tried again, harder this time. "Mr. Allerton, we need to speak to you," he called.

A moment later, the door eased open and a small blonde girl looked out. "Trey says he's taking a nap and can't talk to you right now," she said.

Jamie knelt until she was eye level with the child. "Hello, Ashlyn," she said. "We met once before. My name is Jamie."

Ashlyn stared at her, wide-eyed.

"Can we speak to your mom?" Jamie asked.

"She's napping, too," Ashlyn said. "I'm supposed to be napping, too, but they sent me to answer the door."

Jamie looked up at Wes. They could insist that the child go fetch an adult, but they couldn't compel Trey or Courtney to talk to them.

Wes handed Ashlyn one of his cards. "Give this to Trey and ask him to call me," he said.

Ashlyn took the card and nodded. "Okay."

"Ashlyn, close the door now," Courtney called from the far end of the trailer.

"I have to go now," Ashlyn said and shut the door.

Jamie and Wes returned to the cruiser. "Some days, no one is glad to see you," she said as they headed back to town.

And some days, Wes thought, everyone you met

was hiding something. But he didn't know enough about these people to determine if discovering their secrets would help him to figure out what had happened to Basher Monroe and Cash Whitlow.

Rebecca paced her living room, unable to settle. Wes hadn't returned her call, and she couldn't decide if this was good news—he had nothing to report and he wasn't concerned about Trey Allerton—or if it meant he didn't *want* to talk to her. He was probably busy with other cases and didn't have time to hold her hand. She was supposed to trust that the sheriff's department was doing their job, and Wes would let her know when he had something to report.

But she wasn't the type to sit back and wait. And, truth be told, she wouldn't mind a little hand-holding from the handsome deputy. She hated to admit that—having romantic thoughts about a man right now struck her as inappropriate. But Wes had made her feel less alone in her distress over Cash's disappearance, and that translated into some pretty warm feelings for him.

Did that make her pathetic or just human?

A knock on the door startled her, and she hurried to look outside. A sheriff's department SUV sat at the curb, and Wes stood on her doorstep. She fumbled open the locks and opened the door. "Hello!" she said, smiling in welcome.

"Sorry to stop by so late," he said. "I've been out of phone range all day and just got your message."

"It's not that late." She held the door open wider. "Please, come in."

In the brighter light of her living room, he looked weary, with the slightly slumped shoulders and dull eyes of someone who has worked too many hours and slept too few. "Can I get you some coffee, or water, or something?" she asked.

"I'm okay."

She followed him farther into the room. "Do you have any news?" she asked. "Please, sit down." She sat and he lowered himself to the opposite end of the sofa.

"No news. I spent the day following up some leads and getting nowhere."

"That sounds frustrating."

"All part of the job. I got your message. What did you want to tell me?"

"Something odd happened at work today. I don't know if it means anything or not, but a man came in, Trey Allerton. Our nurse practitioner, Lauren Baker, said I should speak to you about him."

At the name Trey Allerton, Wes sat up straighter. "What did he want?"

"He had a little girl with him, apparently his girl-friend's child, and said he wanted to check her vaccination records. Of course, we couldn't give him that information without the girl's mother's permission, which we didn't have on file. But I really think that was an excuse to talk to me."

"Why do you think that?"

"He knew who I was. He said how sorry he was to

hear about Cash, and asked if we had had any sightings or any theories about what had happened to him. His behavior just struck me as…odd." She felt a little foolish telling him this. It wasn't as if Trey Allerton had really done anything. "I don't know. Maybe he's just one of those people who likes to get the inside scoop on breaking news."

"Trey Allerton was one of the people I was trying to track down today," he said.

Her breath caught and she leaned toward him. "You think he had something to do with Cash's disappearance? Or with Basher's murder?"

"He's leasing part of a ranch in the mountains outside of town and says he plans to build a camp for disadvantaged youth. I wondered if maybe Cash had tried to get a job with him. You mentioned Cash wanted to work with young people, and his fellow climbers said he had talked about getting a job at a camp."

"What did Mr. Allerton say?"

Wes shook his head. "I wasn't able to speak with him. The first time I went by his place, he wasn't there. So Deputy Douglas and I waited and after we knew he was home, we went back. But he refused to come to the door. He sent his girlfriend's daughter to tell us to go away."

"Can he do that—refuse to talk to a law enforcement officer?"

"At this point I don't have any evidence tying him to a crime. I showed his girlfriend, Courtney Baker, the flyer you made, and she said she had never seen

Cash before. Though what you've told me does give me one more reason to try to pin Allerton down."

"I can't imagine why he wouldn't talk to you, unless he is hiding something." She hugged her arms across her chest. "I'm even more creeped out about him now."

Wes's expression hardened. "Did he threaten you or do anything to make you uncomfortable?"

"No. He was perfectly polite. Maybe I was just picking up on Lauren's dislike of him. She's definitely not happy that her brother's widow took up with him."

Wes nodded. "Let me ask you about something else that happened today. It probably doesn't have any connection to Cash, but I need to ask."

"All right."

"There's a gold mine up the road from Trey Allerton's place—the Full Moon Mine. It's operated by a man named Martin Kramer. He says someone has been stealing from him. He described a tall young man in a hoodie and jeans, though he admits he never got a good look at the man's face. Do you think Cash would do something like that?"

"No! Cash doesn't steal. Why would he?"

"Maybe he heard the rumors that Kramer has gold stashed up there."

"Cash doesn't steal," she said again.

"Addicts will do things they wouldn't normally do, including steal to support their habits."

"Cash isn't an addict." She stood. "How many times do I have to tell you that?"

"I believe you," he said, remaining calm. "But I have to consider the possibilities, and ask all the questions, even the hard ones."

She took a deep breath, trying to smother her agitation. "Even when Cash was at his worst, I never heard of him stealing," she said. "I know that doesn't mean he didn't, but even if he was back on drugs—and he's not—but if he was, why target a miner in the middle of nowhere? Why not steal from me or burgle a home or business in town?"

"I agree Kramer seems an odd target," he said. "But I've learned that people sometimes do odd things." He stood. "I've kept you long enough. I'd better get going."

The thought of him leaving left her even more bereft. "You don't have to leave," she said, then, more boldly, "Stay. I could fix us something to eat. Have you had dinner?"

His smile erased most of the weariness from his face and made her feel lighter. "That would be great."

"Come into the kitchen and let's see what I can find," she said.

What she found was chicken and vegetables and tortillas, which she transformed into fajitas while he helped by chopping lettuce and tomato, shredding cheese and setting the table. "I'd offer you a beer or wine," she said as she carried the meal to the table, "but I don't have anything on hand."

"Water is fine." He took his seat and waited until

she was settled before he lifted his water glass. "To the chef," he said.

She solemnly clinked her glass to his, then busied herself making her fajita. It had been a long time since she'd sat across the dinner table from a man. Well, a man other than Cash, who would always be part boy to her. Eating with Wes was different, from her constant awareness of his presence to an awareness of her own movements. She wouldn't have said she was self-conscious around him, simply more conscious of herself as a woman responding to the companionship of this man.

"How long have you lived in Eagle Mountain?" he asked after a moment.

She had to think a moment to find the answer. "Twelve years," she said. "It's hard to believe it's been that long."

"What brought you here, and from where?" he asked.

"From California. The San Diego area. I grew up there. And how I got here is a story you've probably heard a dozen times—I followed a love interest. Things didn't work out with him, but I liked it here and I stayed. What about you? How did you end up with the sheriff's department?"

"The sheriff and I have been friends for a long time," he said. "Since college. I was a few years ahead of him in school, but we shared a lot of the same interests. We kept in touch and he knew I was looking for a change, so he let me know the department was expanding, if I was interested. I was, so…here I am."

"What were you looking for a change from?" she asked. "Or is that too personal a question?"

"I was burning out, working Vice in a big city." He laid down his fork and gave her his full attention. "My last case was a sex-trafficking case. There were children involved. It didn't end well." His voice was even, but she sensed the turmoil behind the words.

"That's terrible," she said. Terrible for him. Terrible for the children. Terrible for a world in which that could happen.

He picked up his fork again. "It was. And now I'm happy to be here, though I imagine some people think of it as running away."

"Some people are wrong," she said.

He chuckled. "You sound so sure of that."

She looked down at her plate. "I guess any job working with the public, you get to see the good and bad sides of people," she said. "Medical practices are privy to people's darker sides, too. In addition to physical ailments, we handle a lot of mental health problems. If you were burned out on your job, you were harming your own health, which meant you couldn't be very effective for others. Now you're here, where I hope you're feeling better, and you've been a big help to me, at least."

"I haven't done anything to help you," he said.

"You've listened and you've believed me, and you're doing everything you can to find and help Cash. Just knowing all that helps me."

He leaned over and covered her hand with his own. "You're an easy person to want to help."

The weight and warmth of his hand, and the strength behind it, filled her with such heat, and a tingle of longing curling up from her middle. She started to turn her hand over, to entwine her fingers with his, but he straightened, pulling his hand away, and resumed eating.

They finished the meal in silence, the absence of conversation not awkward, but humming with tension. She wondered if he was as aware of it as she was.

When the meal was done, he helped collect the dishes and put them in the sink. When he started to turn on the water, she stopped him. "I'll do that later," she said. Then she left her hand on his arm and looked into his eyes, silently asking what he wanted next.

His eyes met hers, then his gaze shifted to her lips. She leaned closer, willing him to kiss her. His eyes darkened, and his grip on her arm tightened. She held her breath, waiting and wanting.

Then he took a step back. "I'd better go," he said, avoiding her gaze. "Thank you for dinner. I'll keep you posted on the case."

And then, before she could protest, he was gone. She stared after him, listening to his footsteps cross the floor, then the door close behind him.

The case. He meant Cash's disappearance. Maybe Basher's murder, too. The thing that had brought them together. Was it now the thing keeping them apart?

Chapter Eight

Wes returned to Trey Allerton's trailer the next morning, determined to talk to the man, but as he passed the gates for Russell Ranch, a black Ford pickup, with Allerton behind the wheel, passed him. Wes pulled onto the side of the road, then turned to follow the truck. He debated switching on his lights to pull the truck over, but decided confronting Allerton at his destination might be more effective.

The destination turned out to be Mountain States Bank. Allerton parked at the curb and went inside the bank. Wes found a space a little down the block. When Allerton emerged from the bank fifteen minutes later, Wes was leaning against the driver's door of the truck. "Hello, Trey," he said. "You and I need to talk."

"I don't have anything to say to you." Allerton stopped in front of Wes, keys in hand. Short of shoving the deputy out of the way, Allerton wasn't going to get into his truck. "Move, so I can leave," he said.

"I just have a few questions." Wes straightened and

took one of the flyers about Cash Whitlow from the pocket of his uniform shirt and unfolded it.

"I've had enough of your questions," Allerton said. "For some reason the sheriff's department has decided I'm guilty of every crime that happens in this county when I haven't done anything wrong. I'm fed up with your harassment."

"I just want to know if you know this young man." Wes held out the flyer.

"I don't know anything about anyone," Allerton said. He tried to move around Wes, but Wes sidestepped to block him.

"Rebecca Whitlow says you were in the medical clinic yesterday, asking about Cash," Wes said.

"I was in the medical clinic with Ashlyn, not that that's any of your business. I'd seen those flyers around town and, like any decent person, I told her how sorry I was her nephew is missing, and that I hope he's found soon."

"Your concern struck her as more than casual," Wes said.

"I can't help what she thinks."

"Cash was talking about getting a job working with young people, teaching them to rock climb," Wes said. "I thought maybe he applied for a job with the camp you're building."

"You know as well as I do that I'm not ready to hire anyone yet."

"So, Cash didn't come to you asking about a job?"

"No. I don't know the guy. I haven't had anything to do with the guy."

"What about Basher Monroe?"

"What is this—throw out every random name on your books and see if it sticks to me? I never heard of him, either."

"Basher was murdered Sunday," Wes said.

"And that has nothing to do with me. None of the deaths you've tried to associate with me have anything to do with me. You people need to do your job and actually investigate crimes instead of making me your convenient universal suspect."

Wes could have left it there, but who knew when he'd have Allerton in this position again? Might as well keep going. "When we spoke to your girlfriend yesterday, we were concerned about her," he said. "She looked like she had a black eye."

Nothing in Allerton's expression changed. "She fell. The ground is pretty rough around our place and she was chasing Ashlyn." He shrugged. "It happens. She'll be fine."

"The deputy with me said it looked like Mrs. Baker had lost weight.

"Courtney looks fine to me. Did she tell you something was wrong?"

"No."

"Then nothing is wrong. And I think we're done."

"Not quite. Your neighbor, Martin Kramer, says someone's been stealing from him," Wes said. "Have you had any trouble at your place?"

"No. And I wouldn't put much stock in anything Kramer said. He's delusional. Or maybe just senile."

"What do you mean?" Wes asked.

"He sees things that aren't there. Or rather he shoots at things that aren't there. He's always firing that shotgun of his at figments of his imagination. I've tried to talk to him about it, but he just shoots at me."

"Have you heard the rumors about him hoarding gold at his place?"

"All he's hoarding are rocks. Everyone knows if those mines really had any gold, the big companies would have taken it out years ago. But hey, if you're looking for a murder suspect, you ought to talk to Kramer about your missing climber. Maybe he shot him."

He shouldered Wes out of the way and jerked open the door to his truck. Wes let him go.

Allerton had an explanation for everything, and Wes had nothing really linking Allerton to any of his cases. Was Allerton right, and the sheriff's department had fixated on him as a convenient suspect? By focusing on him, were they missing out on someone less obvious but truly guilty?

SATURDAY AFTERNOON, Rebecca drove out to Caspar Canyon, an area of rocky cliffs streaked with vermillion and purple from minerals in the rocks. Once a month local climbers gathered here to trade tips and tricks, try out new gear and look for new, ever more challenging routes in what they had termed the Canyon Clinics. Newcomers to the sport came to be tutored by the pros, and professional climbers dropped in to brag about recent conquests and catch up with friends. Cash had been a regular at the clinics, and Rebecca hoped someone there would know more about his activities in the days before he had disappeared.

She hadn't spoken to Wes since their dinner Thursday. She told herself he would contact her if he had any new information about Cash, and she needed time to let her feelings cool off. Clearly he wanted to keep things between them professional. And she respected that, even if part of her longed for more. She hadn't been involved with anyone for more than a year, and she'd been fine with that—until she met Wes. How inconvenient that he also happened to be the deputy investigating Cash's disappearance.

She parked and walked up to the cliff area, and approached a group of climbers. "I wanted to make sure you all had seen the flyer about Cash," she said, handing out copies.

"I was sorry to hear about him," a girl with long red braids—Rebecca thought she went by Zippy—said.

"Do any of you remember him talking about going away?" Rebecca asked. "Or maybe he talked about climbing in a new area? Someplace off the beaten path? I'm worried he went climbing alone and got hurt."

They all shook their heads. "I never heard anything like that," Zippy said. "He wasn't a big talker anyway, but he was really good about helping other people, you know, showing them techniques or suggesting routes."

"And you don't recall seeing his truck parked anywhere recently?" Rebecca asked. "Maybe it didn't really register with you as unusual at the time."

More head shaking. "We're keeping an eye out for him," a young man with an acne-scarred face and a shaved head said.

"Thank you," Rebecca said. "Tell everyone you know about Cash. The more people who are looking for him, the more likely we are to find him."

She turned away, only to almost collide with a tall young man in ragged cargo pants. "Sorry," he said, stumbling back. "I was in a hurry to get to you before you left. Are you Cash's aunt Rebecca?"

"Yes. Do you know something about where Cash might be?"

"I was hoping you knew something." He stuck out his hand. "I'm Payson Fritsch. Cash is a friend of mine. He's been teaching me so much about climbing."

"It's good to meet you, Payson." Rebecca didn't remember Cash ever mentioning Payson. She was beginning to realize how much about her nephew she didn't know.

"I can't believe he just disappeared." Payson shoved his hands deep into the pockets of his shorts and rocked back and forth. He had short-cropped brown hair and beautiful dark brown eyes, with lush lashes Rebecca envied. "We were supposed to meet up here today. He said he was going to show me a new route up the falls." He nodded over his shoulder, toward a trickle of water down the canyon wall. Slick rock showed the path the more forceful waters took during spring runoff.

"So Cash didn't give any indication that he planned to go away somewhere?" Rebecca asked.

Payson shook his head. "No way. I can't believe he's just…gone." He looked as if he might cry.

Rebecca's heart went out to the young man. He looked so forlorn. She tried to find some way to comfort him. "So many people are looking for him," Rebecca said. "I'm really hoping he'll be found soon."

"He was just such a big help to me." Payson wiped at his eyes. "I had a chance to get a job working on this ranch and I was so nervous about the interview that Cash went with me. And Basher—Basher went, too. Cash thought it would be good to have him along because he's so big and kind of intimidating. I guess Cash had a bad feeling about the whole setup from the start."

"When was this?" Rebecca asked.

"Last Saturday." He shook his head.

"Did you get the job?" she asked.

Payson shook his head. "It was just too weird, you know? Cash and I talked it over after the interview and we decided I should probably try for something else. So I got a job at a T-shirt place in town."

"What was weird about it?" she asked.

"First off, the guy who was going to hire me—he said his name was Bart Smith—didn't want to meet at the ranch. We had to meet him at that old, abandoned gas station up on the highway. I'd only talked to him on the phone before that, and when Cash and Basher and I got to the place, the guy—or, at least, I guess it was the guy—was waiting for us. Only he was wearing this really cheesy black wig and a loud Hawaiian shirt. It had, like, alligators on it." He shook his head. "It looked like some kind of costume, not something a rancher would wear."

Rebecca felt cold all over. "How did you find out about this job if you'd never met the man before?"

"He had this card pinned to the bulletin board outside the coin laundry over on South Fifth," Payson said. "I called the phone number on the card and we set up this meeting at the gas station. He said it was more convenient for him."

"Do you still have the card?"

"Sorry. I threw it away."

"What was the job?"

"Just doing odd jobs on the ranch. He said I'd be cutting firewood and clearing brush, and he might want me to ride along when he went to collect money from people who owed him. I thought that was a little weird but, whatever." He shrugged.

"But you decided not to take the job. Why?"

"I just got a bad vibe from the dude—the wig and the loud shirt, and he wore these mirrored sunglasses he didn't take off the whole time we were talking. And then he said he'd pay me eight dollars an hour to work, but I could make more by doing extra jobs for him—but he wouldn't say what the extra jobs were." He stared at the ground and shuffled his feet. "I might still have taken the job, to try it out, you know, if Cash hadn't said it was a bad idea. He said he thought maybe the guy was involved in drugs and he was worried those *extra* jobs might involve selling drugs or something. He said nobody wears a disguise like that unless they have something to hide. Basher agreed that the guy was probably shady."

"And you're sure Cash or Basher didn't know this Mr. Smith?" Rebecca asked.

"No way. They were as weirded out by him as I was." He frowned. "You don't think Smith had anything to do with Cash's disappearance, do you?"

"I don't know," she said. "But I think you should tell the sheriff's department about him and have them check him out."

Payson's eyes widened. "You want me to talk to the cops?"

"One cop. Deputy Wes Landry. He's a good guy." She took out her phone. "Give me your number and I'll have him call you."

"Do you really think it will help Cash?"

"I do."

He gave her his number and she recorded it in her phone. "Thanks for telling me this," she said. "Sometimes it's little things like this that make all the difference." Or so she had heard on TV and read in countless mystery novels.

"Sure. I wish I could do more."

He moved away and she was headed back to her car when someone behind her said, "Hello, Rebecca."

The voice still had the power to stop her in her tracks. She took a deep breath, trying to calm her racing heart, before she turned around. "Hello, Garrett," she said.

Garrett Stokes was a blond beach bum turned rock rat, with the lean, muscular physique of a climber and a ready grin, though he wasn't grinning now. He had been her brother Scott's best friend and frequent climbing partner.

He had also been the man Rebecca had thought she would marry, until it became clear that Garrett had no interest in settling down with one woman, much less her.

"I heard about Cash," he said. "Is there anything I can do?"

A memory flashed through her head of a younger Garrett carrying Cash on his shoulders as the little boy giggled and urged him to run faster. Her heart twisted a little at the thought. They had all been so happy then, before Scott died and her relationship with Garrett withered away. "Have you spoken to Cash lately?" she asked. "In the past couple of weeks?"

"He and I climbed over in Post Office Basin last week," Garrett said.

She blinked. "He never said anything about that to me."

"He probably didn't want to upset you. He knows I'm not your favorite person."

"Oh, Garrett—"

"It's all right, Becca. I probably deserve whatever

your feelings are for me. Anyway, Cash was in a good mood. Full of big plans."

"What kind of plans?"

"He told me he had decided to focus on getting a job working with kids. He was stoked about the idea."

"But you don't know any more?"

Garrett shook his head. "Sorry. I don't."

"Did you know Basher Monroe and Cash were friends?" she asked.

"Yeah. I used to see them together a lot. Basher was a good guy. I heard somebody shot him in that ambulance of his. Did they find out who did that?"

"I don't think so. The manager of Moe's Tavern said Basher and Cash had lunch the day before Basher died. The day before Cash disappeared."

"Huh. Strange timing. Do you think Cash knows something about Basher's murder and is hiding from the killer?"

"I don't know what to think." She wanted someone to make things clear to her—to give her the information that would suddenly reveal all the answers.

"Yeah, well, we're all keeping our eyes and ears open. I'll let you know if I find out anything."

"Thanks." She started to turn away, but he put his hand on your shoulder. "Let's have dinner together," he said. "You look like you could use some cheering up."

She shook her head. "I'm not in the mood."

He took his hand away, all the warmth gone from his eyes. "I take back what I said earlier, about deserving whatever you felt about me. I was never as bad as you made me out to be."

"Garrett, I don't want to have this discussion."

"You were always focused on what I was doing wrong, not what I was doing right." He took a step back. "I've got news for you, Beccs—nobody is perfect, not even you."

He turned and stalked away, leaving her torn between wanting to swear at him and wanting to cry. She hadn't wanted him to be perfect—but she had hoped for a man for whom she wouldn't always be second place in his life.

Chapter Nine

Cash woke to a darkness blacker than any he had ever experienced. He sat up, wincing at the pain in his thigh, and unwrapped the emergency blanket from around himself, the tinfoil-like material crinkling loudly with each movement. He pressed the button to illuminate the display on his watch: 2:54 a.m. Too early to get up and try to go anywhere.

He lay back on his makeshift mattress of pine boughs and closed his eyes again, his mind replaying the events of thc past few days.

The first thing had been that weird interview with Payson and Basher and the man in the bad wig and the alligator shirt, Bart Smith. Cash had had bad vibes about the guy from the beginning, which was one reason he'd suggested Basher come along. Basher wouldn't hurt a flea if he didn't have to, but he was big and strong and looked intimidating.

Cash didn't think it was a coincidence that Bart Smith's initials were B.S. What kind of employer refuses to meet a potential employee at his place of business? Cash had been ready to walk away as soon as he saw the guy's disguise, but he hadn't wanted to embarrass Payson any more than he had to, so he'd stayed to hear the man's spiel.

More bad vibes there. All that talk about extra pay for extra work, but a refusal to say what the work entailed had every nerve in Cash's body saying no. A person with this much to hide was into something bad. Probably drugs. Basher had thought so, too. A ranch in the middle of nowhere was probably the perfect place to manufacture and/or distribute illegal drugs. The man had probably pegged Payson as a naive kid desperate for money, which was sort of true. But the man hadn't figured on Cash having his friend's back.

After Payson turned down the guy's offer, he and Cash and Basher left, but Cash, who was driving, insisted on circling back around and trying to follow the man.

"What are we doing?" Payson asked.

"I want to see if I can figure out who this guy is." He pointed ahead of them, to the smear of mud across the license plate of the white RAV4. "You can bet Bart Smith isn't his real name. And why didn't he want us to know where he lived?"

He kept his truck well back of the RAV4, and was doing a good job of keeping the guy in sight until they turned off on County Road 361. All of a sudden the RAV4 disappeared. Cash guessed the guy had realized he was being followed and turned off into the brush, but even after driving up and down the road three times, they weren't able to figure out where.

The next day Cash had lunch with Basher and told him his plan. "I'm going to find out who this guy is and what he's up to," he said.

"Why do you care?" Basher, who had already eaten all his lunch, stole a French fry off Cash's plate.

"Because—I'm always saying how I want to help kids, you know?"

Basher nodded. "You help them by teaching them to climb, turning them on to how great the sport is."

"Sure. But if we're right and this Smith character is dealing drugs, think how many more kids I'll help by putting him away."

"Who are you now, the DA?" Basher laughed at his own bad joke.

"I'll take my evidence to the sheriff and he can take care of Smith," Cash said. "But I can't just walk into the sheriff's department with a story about a guy with a bad wig. I need evidence."

"How are you going to get evidence?" Basher asked.

"I'm going to drive out to County Road 361 and see if I can find the guy," Cash said. "When I find him, I'm going to watch him. I'm bound to see something suspicious." He shoved back his chair. "Want to come with me?"

"Sure." Basher took out his wallet to pay for lunch. "I don't have anything better to do."

It hadn't taken long to determine there were only

four houses on County Road 361: The Russell Ranch, a faded old single-wide trailer, a yurt and someplace called the Full Moon Mine.

Cash started at the ranch. He pretended to be selling magazine subscriptions. A pregnant woman with a toddler clinging to her legs answered the door. She had long brown hair and a harried look on her face. In the course of trying to sell her nonexistent magazine subscriptions, he learned that she and her husband had only recently taken over operation of the ranch. Her husband showed up about that time and one look told Cash he was too short and stocky to be the man in the wig, so he said goodbye and moved on to the trailer.

A pale blonde woman answered the door here. She would have been really gorgeous if she hadn't looked so tired and sick. She said her husband wasn't around and they didn't need magazines. Cash decided to save time and asked her about her neighbors. Did she think they needed magazines?

"I don't know much about the young couple in the yurt," she said. "Though they're always friendly. But if I were you, I wouldn't go near Mr. Kramer at the Full Moon Mine."

"Why is that?" Cash asked.

"Because he shoots at visitors."

At Cash's blank look, she continued, "He has a shotgun and he shoots at anyone who comes by. He's very paranoid and convinced that everyone is trying to steal from him. He's dangerous, so I'd stay away if I was you."

He thanked her and returned to his truck, where Basher was waiting. He told Basher what the woman had said. "Kramer is our man, I'd bet anything," Cash said as he put the truck into gear and backed out of the driveway.

"Because he's a grouch with a gun, you think he's a drug dealer?" Basher asked.

"He's hiding something," Cash said. "Why else shoot at someone just for turning in your driveway? That's the kind of thing drug dealers do."

"You're the expert."

Cash ignored the comment and drove past the yurt and its accompanying greenhouse, chicken yard and pig pen. Like the trailer, this place looked too poor to belong to someone who was raking in cash from drugs.

He stopped at the sign for the Full Moon Mine, but didn't turn in. "What are you going to do now?" Basher asked.

"We can't just drive up there," Cash said. "If he is Smith, he'll recognize us from the interview with Payson."

"That, and he's liable to shoot us," Basher said.

"We're going to have to sneak in there," Cash said. "Figure out what's going on and take pictures, so I'll have proof to show to the cops."

"I don't know about that," Basher said. "Why don't we drive on out to the old quarry and climb the cliff there? Garrett told me he was out there last week and found a sick new route up the north side."

Cash shook his head. "If you don't want to help me, I'll take you back to your camper and I'll come back out here by myself."

"I didn't say I didn't want to help." Basher squinted up the driveway. "But if you're going to snoop around, you'd be better off doing it after dark. It's a lot harder to hit someone with a shotgun when you can't see them."

So they'd ended up driving out to the quarry after all, and messing around, then Cash went home to eat until almost dark, when he picked up Basher and they drove back to the mine. Cash parked past the end of the road, up above the mine, and they hiked back in the fading light. They lay on their stomachs on a ledge behind Martin Kramer's shack and watched him hauling buckets of rocks from a hole in the hillside that Cash guessed was the entrance to his mine. "I wonder what's underneath all those rocks," he whispered to Basher.

"A mine would be a good place to hide drugs," Basher said. "How are we going to get a closer look?"

"We wait until he's inside and sneak down there. My phone doesn't get a signal up here, but the camera works. We'll take some pictures of what we find and leave. Easy."

"Easy," Basher repeated.

The first part was simple enough. They waited until it got dark and Kramer was inside his shack, then they crept down to the mine entrance and went in. They kept their lights off until they got inside.

Cash had been hoping to find lockers or shelves or some kind of containers filled with illegal drugs, but there were only a bunch of five gallon buckets full of rock. "What's with all this rock?" He picked up a gray chunk about the size of his fist. It was rough and heavy, but it didn't look like anything special.

"I guess that's the ore he's taking out of the mine," Basher said.

"It doesn't look like it's worth anything," Cash said. "I thought the mines around here were supposed to have gold and silver in them."

"I don't know what gold and silver looks like when it's still in the ground," Basher said. "Maybe this is it?"

They moved a little farther into the mine. "There's probably a passage, or another room, or something back here," he called over his shoulder. "Or maybe there's an underground lab." Why hadn't he thought of that before? This place would be perfect for a lab.

"What do you think you're doing?" A light blinded them and an angry voice roared.

Cash couldn't see anything in the glare of that light, but he assumed the person shouting at him was Kramer. He thought the old man was standing in the entrance to the mine, trapping them. Cash was trying to think of something to say to convince the old guy not to kill him when Basher grabbed his arm. "Come with me," Basher muttered. "Now!"

Then he dragged Cash after him as he charged directly at the old guy. Basher almost knocked Kramer over as they ran past. Cash had never run so hard in his life, legs pumping, lungs straining to take in enough oxygen. Kramer fired off a blast from the shotgun behind them, then another. Basher yelped and Cash stumbled. "It's okay!" Basher said. "Go! Go!"

They didn't stop running until they reached Cash's truck. Cash jammed the key in the ignition and the engine roared to life. He raced out of there, the tires kicking up gravel, the truck fishtailing around curves. He didn't care that he was driving way too fast. He would have welcomed being pulled over by a cop, but of course there were no cops out here in the middle of nowhere after dark.

He didn't slow until they were in town. "That was wild," he said and looked over to Basher.

Only then did he realize his friend was hurt. Basher lay back against the seat, his face gray, eyes closed, one hand pressed to his side. Cash slammed on the brakes and pulled to the side of the road, just past the grocery store. "Basher! Are you okay?"

Basher opened his eyes, then lifted the hand from his side and looked down. Cash stared at the dark wet patch spreading across Basher's T-shirt. "Dude, did he shoot you?" he asked.

"I don't think it's that bad," Basher said. He clapped his hand back over his side. "Just take me back to the camper."

"If you're shot, I need to take you to the hospital."

"No! No hospital!"

He sounded like he meant it, but come on! "If you

won't let me take you to the hospital, we should at least go to the sheriff's office," Cash said. "That old guy can't go around just shooting at people."

"Except we were trespassing on his property after dark," Basher said. "The cops will probably want to lock us up, not him."

"Basher, come on."

"No!" The anger behind the single word made Cash shrink back. "No cops and no doctors," Basher said. "Just take me to the camper. I'll be fine."

So Cash took him to the old ambulance he had transformed into a pretty awesome camper. Basher groaned as he slid out of the truck, and Cash came around and helped him limp into the camper, where he sank onto his bunk. "Let me see," Cash said, pointing to Basher's side.

Basher pulled up his shirt to reveal an angry puncture wound, red and seeping around the edges, though it had almost stopped bleeding. "I thought there'd be lots of pellets from a shotgun," Cash said.

"I guess just one pellet got me. Help me strip off this shirt. I'm just going to go to bed. I'll be fine in the morning."

"Should we maybe clean it up and bandage it?" Cash asked. "In case it starts bleeding again?"

"Sure. We could do that. The first-aid kit is in the bathroom."

Cash found the first-aid kit and, with a lot of swearing from Basher, managed to clean up the wound and tape some gauze over it. It seemed to be bleeding more now, but Basher insisted he was okay. "I just want to get some sleep," he said.

"Okay." Cash stood. "I'll check on you in the morning, see if you need anything."

Basher reached out and grabbed Cash's arm, hard enough to hurt. Cash tried to wrench free, but Basher held tight. "No cops," he said. "Don't tell anybody about this. Not even your aunt."

"Why not?"

Basher winced. "I can't risk having my name in the paper. You know how they always print that sheriff's report that lists all the calls they went on. There are people—bad people—that I don't want seeing my name in there and coming after me."

Was Basher delirious or something? "What are you talking about? What people?"

"Just some people I used to know. In Colorado Springs."

"I thought you were from Maryland."

"I'm from Maryland, but I spent some time in the Springs. It doesn't matter. I just can't risk anyone seeing my name in the paper and coming looking for me. Understand?"

Cash didn't really understand, but he nodded.

"Promise you won't say anything to anyone," Basher said.

"I promise," Cash said.

Basher lay back on the bunk and closed his eyes. He looked pretty awful, but maybe he was just tired. "I'll be fine," Basher said. "See you later."

Cash left him to sleep and went home, managing to slip in without running into his aunt Rebecca. It wasn't until he got into his room that he realized he had blood all over his shirt. He stripped off all his clothes and hid them at the bottom of the pile in his closet. He'd deal with them later. He took a shower and went to bed. Basher didn't answer the text he sent the next morning, but Cash figured he was either asleep or had gone in to work the early shift at the café. Cash decided to go by himself to spy on Kramer again.

Big mistake. Now he was hurt, too. His truck had disappeared and he'd lost his phone. Had that really been almost a week ago? That's what his watch told him, but he had no memory of much of that time. Aunt Rebecca was probably really upset with him by now. And really worried. He hoped she hadn't called his mom, but he was sort of hoping she had contacted the sheriff. He liked to think that somebody was looking for him.

He hoped they were. He didn't know how many more days he could last up here on his own.

Chapter Ten

"Next up, we've got some updates on the Basher Monroe murder investigation," Travis addressed the gathered deputies Saturday morning. "Wes, let's start with the analysis of the blood found on the shirt belonging to Cash Whitlow."

"The state lab says the blood found on the shirt is a match for Basher Monroe," Wes said. That wasn't the news Rebecca wanted to hear.

"How much blood are we talking about?" Deputy Dwight Prentice asked.

"Several ounces," Wes said.

"So we're not talking a cut finger," Gage said. "It's enough to put Cash with Basher at or near the time he was first shot, since the ME's report says the second shot—the head wound—didn't really bleed."

"Did Cash shoot Basher?" Jamie asked.

"The blood on Cash's shirt wasn't a spatter pattern," Wes said. "And in any case, the ME said most of Basher's blood loss was internal bleeding. I talked to Dr. Collins again after I got this report from the state lab, and he said the external blood loss from Basher's wound was blood seeping out, not gushing. In his opinion, in order for blood to soak into Cash's shirt, he either had to lay in a pool of blood that had already seeped out of Basher or be positioned right up against him."

"So, maybe when he was helping Basher into his bunk at the camper," Gage said.

Wes nodded. "Something like that. I'm wondering if Basher's death is somehow related to a conversation Jamie and I had with Martin Kramer on Thursday. He told us someone had been trying to steal from him—a young man in a hoodie. Kramer admitted to firing on the man with his shotgun. He said he only had birdshot in the gun, but what if he was lying about that?"

"When did this occur?" Travis asked.

"He said it was Monday," Wes said.

"That doesn't match up with Basher's time of death," Gage pointed out.

"But if Kramer heard that Basher had died from a gunshot wound, he might have put two and two together and lied to protect himself," Wes said.

"You and Jamie question Kramer again," Travis said. "And talk to Rebecca Whitlow again. Maybe Cash mentioned wanting to climb on those cliffs above the Full Moon Mine."

"Yes, sir." Wes hadn't exactly been avoiding Rebecca since their dinner Thursday evening, but he had thought it a good idea to put a little distance between them, to try to rein in his feelings. She was a beautiful, interesting woman and under other circumstances, he wouldn't have hesitated to act on the attraction that simmered between them. But working a case that involved someone you cared about complicated things in so many ways. His last relationship had ended badly when the woman he was seeing became part of the investigation. She'd expected more of him than he'd been able to give. What if Cash Whitlow was never found? Would Rebecca blame him and end whatever developed between them?

But he couldn't avoid her altogether. He'd promised to tell her about the lab results on the bloody shirt she had found, and now he needed to quiz her about Cash's familiarity with the area around Kramer's mine.

"Dwight, you talk to every business in town that sells ammunition," Travis said. "See if any of them sold 12-gauge slugs to Kramer. The rest of us will keep pressing the local climbers for information about Cash. If Kramer was firing at anyone who approached his place and Cash and Basher were up there for whatever reason, there's a chance Basher isn't the only one who was hit by one of his shots."

REBECCA WAITED UNTIL she was home to call Wes. "Hello, Rebecca," he answered. "What can I do for you?"

He sounded glad to hear from her—or was she reading too much into a simple greeting? "I spoke to some more climbers this morning," she said. "I learned some things you need to know."

"I need to talk to you, too," he said.

About Cash? she wanted to ask, but stopped herself. Why else would he sound so grim? She tried to brace herself for the worst. "All right. Do you want me to come to the sheriff's department? Or you could come here." Whatever he had to say, she would rather not hear it in a public place.

"I can come to you. About 12:15?"

"All right." She was grateful he didn't make her wait much longer. Even so, by the time he arrived she was jittery with nerves. She tried to determine how bad his news might be by the expression on his face, but he revealed nothing. She supposed law enforcement officers were schooled in not showing their emotions. "Come in," she said, then as soon as she closed the door, "What did you need to talk to me about?"

"We got back the results of the lab tests on the shirt you found," he said. "The blood on it is a match for Basher Monroe."

All the air left her lungs and she sank onto the sofa. "How?" she asked.

"We don't know. It's possible Cash was with Basher when he was shot."

"Cash wouldn't have shot Basher." She looked up at him, silently pleading for him to believe her. "He wouldn't. Cash isn't violent. He doesn't own a gun. I don't think he's ever shot one." Maybe she was wrong about that. There was so much she didn't know about her nephew.

Wes sat down on the sofa, only a few inches from

her. "It's possible Cash got the blood on his shirt when he tried to help Basher."

"Yes. That has to be it. He would try to help his friend."

"Did he say anything about meeting up with Basher on Saturday?"

"No. We hardly talked that day. And I tried to give him privacy and not be overly nosy about his comings and goings."

"Did Cash ever talk about climbing in the area at the end of County Road 361?"

She frowned. "No. Is that a new climbing area? I'm not familiar with it."

"There are some cliffs there. They're not very accessible, but maybe that would be an attraction for him—some place no one else was climbing."

"I never heard him talk about it. Why? Do you think he was there?"

"It's near Martin Kramer's place. And remember, I told you he said he saw a young man in a hoodie and jeans in that area a few days ago," Wes said.

She sank back. "That description could be anyone."

"We're following up on everything, no matter how small."

"Of course." She smoothed her hands down her thighs. "I appreciate it."

"You said you had something to tell me about?" he prompted after a moment.

"Oh, yes." She tried to bring her mind back to the present, to pull away from the dark pit of imagining all of the terrible things that might have happened to Cash. "I went out to Caspar Canyon this afternoon and met a climber you really need to talk to. His name is Payson Fritsch and I have his phone number."

"Why do I need to talk to him?"

"He was with Cash last Saturday. Cash went with him to meet a man called Bart Smith. Smith was wearing an obviously fake black wig and a shirt with alligators on it."

"Was it Basher Monroe?"

"No. Basher Monroe was with them."

"How did they know Smith?"

"They didn't know him. Payson told me he had seen a card tacked up at the coin laundry, advertising for help to work on a ranch. He called the number and this Bart Smith told him to meet at the old gas station out on the highway. You know, the one that's been closed for years?"

Wes nodded. "I know the place. Why not meet at the guy's ranch?"

"Apparently Cash thought that was suspicious, too, so he and Basher went with Payson to meet the guy. I guess Cash has been mentoring Payson, and maybe he was protective of him. Payson said they asked Basher to come with them because Basher was big and intimidating." She shook her head. "I had no idea. I mean, I thought Cash told me everything, but I'm finding out there's so much I don't know."

"What about Smith?" Wes prompted.

She sighed. "Apparently he offered Payson the job,

but he also offered extra pay for extra work—but he wouldn't say what the work was. The guys didn't like the sound of any of it, so Payson turned down the job. Cash told Payson he didn't think Smith was the man's real name and that wearing a disguise and refusing to give details meant the man had something to hide. Cash thought he might be involved in drugs or something."

Her eyes met Wes's. "I'm wondering if Cash got involved with this man somehow—not using drugs again, but maybe he confronted the man about preying on kids like Payson?"

"I'll talk to Payson. And we'll try to track down Smith."

"Now I'm really scared for Cash." Rebecca buried her face in her hands. "I just feel so helpless and alone." She fought to keep back tears. She needed to be strong, for Cash.

Wes put his arm around her and drew her close and she leaned against him, saying nothing, taking comfort from his strength.

The buzz of his phone shattered the stillness between them. "I'd better get that," he said and shifted away.

She stood and went into the bathroom, determined to pull herself together. Maybe Cash had gone climbing in that area Wes was talking about. And maybe they would find him soon, and he would be all right.

When she emerged from the bathroom, Wes was waiting for her. "They've found a truck," he said. "We don't know for sure yet, but it sounds like it could be Cash's."

"Where is it? Who found it?" *Why isn't Cash with it?*

"It's in a ravine in the national forest. A wildlife officer found it. That's all I know. I'm going out there now to take a look."

"Let me come with you."

She hadn't realized she had gripped his arm until he laid his hand over hers. She pulled away and stood straighter, forcing herself to appear calm and rational, though inside she felt anything but. "I can identify the truck, and tell you if any of Cash's things are missing."

"It might not even be Cash's truck," he said. "Apparently the license plates are missing. We'll have to check the vehicle ID number."

"I'll know his truck. And if it isn't his, I'll know that much sooner. We all will." *Can't you see how sitting here doing nothing is making things that much worse?* But she didn't want to beg him to take her.

"All right." He took his keys from his pocket. "But try not to get your hopes up."

Hope was the only thing keeping her going right now. That, and the belief that he was doing everything he could to help. One day she would find the words to tell him how much that meant. One day, when Cash was found and life could move forward again.

"THE LICENSE PLATES are missing, but the description fits the one on the bulletin we received." Wes stood with wildlife officer Nate Hall in a narrow canyon below Dakota Ridge, contemplating a gray Toyota Tacoma that lay on its side up against the trunk of a cottonwood tree, the roof caved in and the front quarter panel smashed. Every window in the vehicle was broken, and a tree branch poked through the roof of the camper top.

Getting to this spot had required a two-mile hike from the end of a narrow Jeep road, then a steep climb down. Wes had tried to persuade Rebecca to wait for him in the parking area, but he hadn't been surprised when she refused, and she hadn't balked when confronted with the climb or the wrecked truck, which didn't look as if anyone in it could have survived. She had only turned a little paler and pressed her lips tightly together before taking a deep breath and saying, "That's Cash's truck. I'm sure of it."

"This is Rebecca Whitlow, Cash Whitlow's aunt," Wes said to Nate. He walked closer to the wreck and peered into the camper. A tangle of ropes and what might have been a sleeping bag were visible in the dim interior. He looked back over his shoulder at Nate. The big blond was responsible for enforcing game laws across a wide swath of the county. "How did you ever find it out here?" he asked.

"A hiker saw the ruts of the tires veering off the old Jeep road up top and got curious," Nate said. "He spotted the truck from the ridge and reported it when he got back within phone range. I was supposed to be in this area today checking on some cameras we have out as part of some research into the local lynx population, so I agreed to check it out. The hiker was smart enough to note the GPS coordinates, so I didn't have any trouble locating the wreck."

Rebecca picked her way over to stand beside Wes. "That looks like climbing gear in the back," she said. "And Cash has a sleeping bag like that." She looked around them, at the stacked boulders and old tree trunks piled up like children's toys. "But where is Cash?"

Wes took her elbow and encouraged her to come with him, away from the vehicle. They rejoined Nate. "We'll get the VIN to verify, but I'm sure she's right," he said. He looked up the slope to the craggy ridge. "How far is it up there?"

"Three hundred yards or so," Nate said. "You can see the path the truck took coming down by the broken bushes." He pointed, indicating the scar of broken limbs and dislodged rocks that marked the truck's trajectory.

Wes studied the ground around the vehicle, which looked undisturbed. The driver's side of the Toyota was wedged tight against the trunk of the cottonwood, and a large boulder would have made it difficult to open the passenger door wide enough to exit. Yet there was no one in the cab of the truck.

"No sign of the driver," Nate said. He cast a wary glance at Rebecca but continued, "No blood, no cut seat belts and no key in the ignition."

Wes looked up the slope again. "So how did the truck get down here? Did someone push it over?"

"That's what I think," Nate said. "You'll want some forensics guys to look at those tracks. Maybe they'll find some shoe impressions. But once you get off the Jeep trail, there's a pretty good incline. If someone was parked on the side of the trail, it wouldn't take that much to start the truck rolling toward the edge."

Rebecca gasped.

"If Cash Whitlow wasn't in the truck, where is he?" Wes asked.

"I've already called for a search," Nate said. "There's nothing to indicate he was in the vehicle when it went over, but this is pretty rough territory, so…"

He left the sentence unfinished, but Rebecca completed the thought. "But he could be out here anywhere, under fallen leaves or rock fall or brush."

"If he is, we'll find him," Wes said. He believed they would do everything in their power to do so, but was he overestimating their capabilities? This was difficult terrain, with wild animals. What if Cash had crawled away somewhere to hide? The more he thought about it, the more monumental the task seemed. But a lot of police work was about confronting monumental tasks, creating a whole picture out of tiny fragments. The challenge appealed to him most of the time.

Wes was taking more photographs of the scene when a forensics team and the search-and-rescue crew arrived. "We're almost positive this is Cash Whitlow's truck," he told the SAR captain, a rangy bearded man who introduced himself as Tony Meisner. "We don't have any evidence that he was in the truck when it went off the cliff, but we need to make sure."

Meisner nodded. "We've done these kinds of searches before. With luck, we'll find him or some indication of where he might be."

Forensics would comb the area as well, then arrange to get the mangled vehicle out of the canyon. "It could take a few days," Gage, who was heading up the team, said. "It's going to take some maneuvering."

Rebecca, who had taken up a position nearer the truck, rejoined him. "Search and Rescue is going to comb the area," Wes said. "They've had experience with this kind of search before."

She nodded. "Everyone is working so hard. I wish there was more I could do."

"We'd better go and leave them to it," he said.

She followed him back the way they had come. The climb up was harder, not merely because of the steepness, but because they had to leave this place with so many questions still unanswered.

Chapter Eleven

Wes drove Rebecca home. They didn't say much on the drive. She stared out the side window and tried to imagine what had happened to Cash. Was he out there, alone and hurt? Or was he already dead?

Wes parked at the curb in front of her house and they sat in silence for a moment. "Do you want to come in?" she asked, then before he could answer she shook her head. "Of course not, you have to get back to work. I know you have so much to do." She opened the door and started to climb out of the cruiser.

"I can come in for a few minutes," he said. "I want to take another look at Cash's room."

Right. This was all about the case.

She unlocked the door and they went inside. Stopping only to drop her purse on the table by the door, she led the way back to Cash's room. As spartan and cold as the last time Wes had seen it. "There's so little of his personality here," she said. "Nothing to tell us what he was thinking or feeling."

"He may not have planned this out." Wes picked

up one of the books on the dresser, then set it down again. "We just don't know."

"Come on." He took her arm and guided her out of the room. "We're not going to find anything here."

"I've been going over and over all this in my head," she said as they moved toward the living room. "We know that last Saturday afternoon Cash and Basher and Payson met with Bart Smith. The next day Basher and Cash had lunch together at Moe's Tavern. Sometime after that on Sunday, Basher was injured, probably by the shot that eventually killed him. Cash got Basher's blood on his shirt and left the shirt here, before leaving the house again Monday morning. Basher died Monday afternoon. And sometime after he left here on Monday, Cash's truck ended up in that ravine." She shook her head. "If Basher was hurt, why didn't Cash tell anyone about it? Why didn't he tell me when he came home Sunday night? And what was he doing out there near that ravine anyway?"

"Maybe he went to climb."

"It's not a place for climbing. The cliffs are more clay than rock, or too obstructed by trees, or not vertical enough. And Cash's climbing gear was in the back of the truck. I can't be certain it was all there, but I think it was. You said you didn't think Cash was in the truck? What makes you think that?"

"The keys weren't in the truck's ignition," he said. "The truck was wedged between a big cottonwood and a boulder. If someone was in there, they wouldn't have been able to open the doors to get out, and the way the roof was smashed, he wouldn't have been able to crawl out the windows, either. There wasn't any obvious blood, and no sign that the seat belt had been cut or broken. Search and Rescue is out there going over the area, but I think if Cash had been thrown from the vehicle on the way down, we'd have found him or some indication that he'd been there."

She put a hand over her mouth and dropped to the sofa. "Where is he?" she asked. "What's happened to him?"

He sat beside her, his arm strong around her. She leaned into him, and breathed in his scent. All this worry had left her with little energy for anything else. And no more willingness to continue to fight her attraction to this man. She lifted her head and met his gaze, and saw her desire reflected back to her. She slid her hand around to the back of his neck and gently pulled his mouth to hers.

He kissed her with the intensity of a man who had decided that he, too, was done with holding back. His lips were firm but tender, and she responded hungrily, greedy to taste and feel. She leaned into him, pressing her breasts against the hard wall of his chest—*body armor*, she thought, and smoothed her hands across the muscles of his biceps. After so much time holding back, she felt reckless. He was the first to pull away. "This could be a really bad idea," he said.

"Or a really good one." She crawled into his lap, straddling him, and kissed him again.

He cupped her face in his hands and looked into

her eyes. "You've had a rough day," he said. "You're emotionally vulnerable now and…"

"And I want this." She splayed her hand across his chest, over his heart. "I want to be with you. Nothing complicated. Just that."

The doubt she had seen in his eyes fled, and he pulled her close once again. "Give me a minute to call in to the office," he said.

"I'll wait in the bedroom."

Wes dialed the sheriff's direct line at the office, but instead the office manager, Adelaide Kincaid, answered the phone. "I need to take a couple hours personal time," he said.

"Oh? Is everything all right?"

"Everything's fine. Just something I need to see to."

"So you're signing out of your shift two hours early? I'll make note of that, but what should I put as the reason?"

This was exactly the kind of grilling he'd been hoping to avoid. "Just note that it's for personal time. I'll be back on shift Monday. Or sooner if I'm needed."

"Will do, Deputy."

He hung up before Adelaide could question him further. And before he could overthink this whole thing and leave. But he didn't think he was strong enough to do that. He'd wanted Rebecca almost from the moment they met and if she wanted to be with him now—for sex, or comfort, or for whatever reason—he wasn't going to deny them that.

She was waiting for him in the bedroom, still

dressed but seated on the edge of the bed. Her eyes met his when he walked into the room and he felt the impact of that gaze to his core. She held up her arms. "Come here."

He had thought she would kiss him again, but instead she began undoing the buttons of his uniform shirt. Her fingernails scraped against the rough surface of his body armor. "Let me help," he said and reached down to unbuckle his duty belt, then laid it carefully to one side. She finished unbuttoning his shirt, then he stripped it off and removed the body armor as well.

"You must feel ten pounds lighter now," she said.

"Just about." He slid his hands beneath her T-shirt, trailing his fingers across the soft silk of her stomach, then moving up to slide his thumbs under the band of her bra. She reached back and unfastened the strap, then peeled off bra and shirt together, revealing full breasts that he had to stare at a moment before reaching for her once more.

They fell back on the bed together, wriggling out of their clothes and laughing—over the awkwardness of the moment, with a little nervousness, and with a lot of joy. When at last he pulled her, naked, on top of him, he was ready to put aside thoughts of everything and everyone but her.

There was always an urgency with a new lover, that desire to see everything, do everything, feel everything. But he was old enough to know the value in taking things slow. They'd only have one first time. It didn't have to be the best, but it ought to mean something. Would she think he was overly sentimental if he told her that? After all, men weren't supposed to be so focused on feelings—said who?

Then she straddled him and his mind finally shut up and instinct took over. They set about discovering each other—the soft gasp she gave when he pulled the tip of her breast into his mouth, and the lightning bolt of need that rocketed through him when she wrapped her hand around the length of his erection. She liked when he feathered kisses over her belly, and he growled with pleasure at the feel of her fingernails raking lightly down his back. The low chuckle in the back of her throat when he stroked the satiny skin at the top of her thigh sent a quiver through him, and when she wrapped her legs around his waist and pulled him tight against her, he wanted to shout in triumph.

He loved her with his hands, and with his mouth, and finally with his whole body, sliding over and into her as she gripped his hips and kept her gaze steady on his eyes, saying so much without a single word. He kept watching her, making note of what pleased her, and what filled her expression with a kind of awe, and then release as her climax shuddered through her. This time he did shout as his own release followed. He felt needed and powerful and…whole. For the first time in a long time.

REBECCA WOKE TO dim light, aware of movement on the bed beside her. Wes was sitting up on the side of the bed, reaching for his pants. "Do you have to go?" she asked, then immediately regretted the question. She would not be a clinging woman. And he had a life apart from her, and a job that made demands on him at all hours.

"I don't have to go," he said. "But I thought I might fix us something to eat."

They made sandwiches, her in her robe, him clad only in his uniform trousers, a very pleasant sight across the kitchen table from her. He had messy hair and a five-o'clock shadow and looking at him, she couldn't stop smiling.

"I want to tell you why I left St. Louis," he said when all that was left of their meal was a few crumbs and some crumpled napkins.

Her first instinct was to protest that he didn't have to, but that wasn't right. If he wanted to tell her, she wanted to know. "All right."

He stared down at his hands, flat on the table in front of him. "I had a case. A tough one. I was working Vice and we were trying to track down the head of a pedophile ring. We had caught some of the people he was peddling kiddie porn to, but we needed to locate the man making the films. I thought we had a good lead, and I followed it for months—but I was wrong. And in the time I wasted, that many more kids were abused by that scum."

"I'm sure you did your best," she said, wishing she could find better words to lessen the pain behind his words.

"But my best wasn't good enough. When that happens—it makes you start questioning your job. Maybe you're not the right person to do this, if your best falls so short."

She waited, forcing herself to remain silent. To give him time. He looked older, the light over the table deepening the grooves on either side of his mouth, hooding his eyes so she could no longer read his expression. She felt privileged, seeing him like this—a strong man allowing himself to be vulnerable.

"We were working the case of a missing child," he said after a moment. "When we spotted the girl in one of the films, we tracked down her mother. That's how she and I got involved." He shook his head.

When he said nothing more, she couldn't bear it. "What happened?" she asked.

"We finally caught the guy. It took too long and too many people were hurt before it was over."

"What happened to the daughter?"

"She died. She killed herself."

"Oh." She put one hand to her mouth, trying to stifle the cry, and another over her heart, where pain stabbed for this child and this woman she didn't even know. And for Wes, carrying all of this with him.

"The mother blamed me for not saving her."

"Wes—"

"Yeah, well, I blamed myself, too."

"It's a terrible thing to happen." She tried to choose her words carefully, not wanting to resort to cliché, but unwilling to remain silent. "But you're only one man. You can't make the whole world right. And you did find the man. Think how many children you saved because you did stop him."

He nodded. "You're right. It's what I try to live with now, but I don't think I'd be human if I ever completely shook the guilt."

"So you decided to come to Eagle Mountain." She was anxious to shift the conversation to what she hoped were happier times.

"I wanted out of Vice. Away from the kind of crime I like to imagine only happens in big cities. I know that's foolish. Some of the people we arrested for buying those kiddie porn films were from small towns. I know no place is immune."

"But Eagle Mountain doesn't have a vice squad," she said. "Things are a little…tamer here. Most of the time."

He nodded.

"What do you think, now that you're here?" she asked. "Are you bored because it's not the fast pace you're used to?"

"No. I was ready to have a job that didn't consume my whole life." He shifted, the chair creaking. Maybe it was just the angle of light as he changed position, but he seemed less burdened now. "Since I've moved here, I've gotten back into fly fishing and photography. I go hiking, and I'm getting to know people in town."

He leaned across and took her hand.

She held his hand and his gaze. "I'm not going to

blame you if you don't find Cash," she said. "Or if you don't find him alive." She had to face that possibility.

His grip tightened. "Grief changes people," he said. "You might not be able to help yourself."

"I won't blame you."

"Don't make promises you don't know you can keep."

"And don't worry about something that hasn't happened yet. That will never happen." She stood and pulled him close. "None of us can predict the future, so let's just be grateful for what we have. Let's enjoy now. I intend to enjoy it a lot."

She took his hand and led him back to bed. Whatever bad happened tomorrow or next week, she would have this good to balance it. She knew life didn't really work that way, but it was a nice thought, and she was determined to hang on to every good thing she could. She would hang on to Wes, as long as he would let her, and not worry about ever having to let go.

"GOOD MORNING, DEPUTY," Adelaide greeted Wes when he arrived at work Monday morning. "Did you enjoy your afternoon off?"

"It was fine." He started past her, but she stopped him.

"Deputy Landry, could you come here a moment?" she asked.

He turned toward her. "Yes?"

She crooked her finger, motioning him to come closer. When he reached her desk, she leaned toward him and spoke in a low voice. "Just a word of advice. It's always good to remember that this is a small town. People notice things."

Why did he suddenly feel like a kid caught out playing hooky by the principal? "What are you getting at?"

"Unless you want the whole town knowing you spent Saturday afternoon and evening at Rebecca Whitlow's house, it would be a good idea to park around back."

He wasn't one for blushing, but now his face burned. "I wasn't—" he began. Wasn't what? Wasn't skipping out of work early to make love with the woman whose missing nephew he was supposed to be looking for?

"Shh." Adelaide put a finger to her lips. "We're all adults here. It's just a good idea to be discrete.

He blew out a breath, part relief and part exasperation. "Thanks. I'll keep that in mind."

At his desk, he started sifting through the various bulletins and reports that had come in since yesterday. He was reading through a bulletin about a string of thefts in a neighboring county when Gage added a new report to the pile. "You'll want to read this one," Gage said.

"The FBI found a match for Basher Monroe's prints."

"Oh?" Wes picked up the paper.

"Basher's real name isn't Benjamin Monroe," Gage said. "It's Bradley. Benjamin is his younger brother."

Wes stopped reading and looked up. "What else?" Gage obviously wanted to tell him.

"Benjamin hasn't had so much as a traffic ticket," Gage said. "Bradley, on the other hand, was in and out of court and local jail in Colorado Springs on a string of petty theft and drug charges." He leaned over and tapped the paper. "It says here that the last time he was charged, he made a deal to testify against his supplier, but skipped town before he could do so."

"Was he running from the supplier, the cops or both?" Wes asked.

"I don't know, but his murderer may have been settling an old score. Or maybe he was back to dealing. Maybe Cash Whitlow was in it with him."

Chapter Twelve

"If you're calling about my brother, I haven't seen or spoken to him in at least eighteen months," Benjamin Monroe, reached at his office in Maryland, said after he and Wes exchanged hellos.

"What makes you think I'm calling about your brother?" Wes asked.

"You're a sheriff's deputy from Colorado. Last I heard, Bradley was in Colorado, and he's had his share of trouble with the law. It's one of the reasons I've distanced myself from him."

"When was the last time you saw your brother?"

"Thanksgiving, year before last. He came home for a few days. He said he was going to make a fresh start, stay away from drugs and out of trouble. He talked about fixing up a camper and doing some traveling, but then I didn't hear from him again, so I thought maybe that didn't work out for him."

"You weren't worried when you didn't hear from him?"

The man on the other end of the line let out an audible sigh. "Bradley was a grown man, from a good family, with a good education. He had all the same advantages I did, but he repeatedly made bad choices in his life. You can only worry about someone like that for so long before it's too exhausting. My parents might not say that, but it's true for me. When Bradley ran out of money or needed real help, I figured he'd call. But you're calling instead, so tell me what's wrong."

"I'm sorry to have to tell you that your brother is dead, Mr. Monroe."

A heavy silence greeted this news. Wes waited, and Benjamin finally cleared his throat. "What happened?"

"He was murdered. Shot in the ambulance he had converted to a camper."

"Shot?" Another throat clearing. "What happened? I mean, who would shoot him? When did this happen?"

"Monday, the twenty-second. Were you aware that your brother was using identification that belonged to you? That's why it took us a few days to determine his real identity and track you down."

"My…my driver's license!"

"You knew your brother had your driver's license?"

"No. I thought I'd lost it. Right after that Thanksgiving, the last time I saw him. I was doing some shopping and thought it had fallen out of my wallet. I replaced it right away. But Bradley had it?"

"He did. Though he went by the nickname Basher."

"Basher, huh?"

"Did you and your brother look alike?" Wes asked.

"We did. When we were children, people some-times mistook us for twins. And when I was in high school and he was in college, I'd sometimes use his ID to get into clubs while I was still underage. I sup-pose that's where he got the idea of using my driver's license. I'm sorry, what town did you say you were calling from?"

"Eagle Mountain. It's a small town in southwest-ern Colorado."

"Last I heard, Bradley was in Colorado Springs. What was he doing in Eagle Mountain?"

"This area is popular with rock climbers. Basher was part of that community. You mentioned your brother's previous run-ins with the law. What can you tell me about those?"

"Surely you've accessed his record by now."

"I'd welcome any information you can provide. The records don't go into a great deal of detail."

"Bradley has been involved with drugs off and on since college. Probably before then, but his first arrest for possession happened when he was a junior in col-lege. After that, he become more heavily involved and dropped out of school. My parents paid for in-patient rehab and then they persuaded a friend in Colorado Springs to hire him. They thought removing him from his former friends and suppliers would help him stay clean, but it didn't work that way. He fell back into using, and then apparently selling drugs. My parents spent a great deal of money trying, mostly successfully, to keep him out of jail. He had just gotten out of jail that Thanksgiving when he came home to visit. He said this time he was really going to stay clean. I didn't believe him, but my parents wanted to. I'm sure they gave him money—and then we never heard from him again. Do you think his death had anything to do with drugs?"

"The toxicology report showed no drugs in his system," Wes said. "And we didn't find any illegal drugs in his camper."

"Wow. That almost makes this harder to take. But if he really was clean, why didn't he stay in touch? Not hearing from him, not knowing where he was— it hurt my parents so much."

"Mr. Monroe, do you think it's possible your brother was hiding from someone?"

Another long pause. "Mr. Monroe?"

"Maybe. I don't know. I mean, my impression is there are some pretty nasty people involved in drug trafficking. And you say he was living in a small town, using my name instead of his own. That sounds like someone who might have been hiding."

"Were you aware that the last time he was arrested, he agreed to testify against the people who were supplying him with drugs to sell in exchange for a more lenient sentence?"

"No, I didn't know that. We never talked about his criminal activities."

"So you don't know who his suppliers were?"

"No. Maybe the police in Colorado Springs have an idea."

"I'll be talking to them," Wes said. "One last question—did your brother ever mention a man named Bart Smith to you?"

"No. That name doesn't sound familiar. Like I said, we never talked about that part of his life. I didn't want to know."

"Thank you, Mr. Monroe. If I have more questions, I'll be in touch."

"What happens now?" Monroe asked. "I mean, to Bradley…to his body? My parents will want to know."

"I'll contact you again when we release his body and belongings," Wes said. "I'm sorry for your loss. If you or your parents have any other questions or think of anything that might be helpful to our investigation, you can reach me at this number."

He ended the call, then stared down at the notes he had made while he had been talking to Monroe. It sounded as if Basher had kept his promise to stay out of trouble and stay clean. He had no more encounters with the law—not even a traffic ticket—for the past eighteen months, and no one they interviewed had mentioned anything about drugs. But Basher Monroe had behaved like a man in hiding—using his brother's driver's license, having no fixed address and taking the kinds of low-wage jobs that didn't involve background checks. That seemed to point to the person he was hiding from having found and killed him.

But it didn't explain him being shot twice, at different times. And it didn't account for Cash Whitlow's involvement. Had Cash merely been in the wrong place at the wrong time, or was he somehow more deeply involved?

REBECCA WELCOMED THE distraction of a busy Monday morning at the medical clinic. When she arrived at work, she collected six messages from the answering service and others quickly followed, along with three people who showed up to see the doctor or nurse practitioner whenever they could be worked in. As well as regular appointments, she had the weekend's mail to open and emails to be answered or forwarded to other staff members for answers. Sometimes these mornings overwhelmed her, but today she was grateful for a reason not to think about Cash.

Or about Wes. Thoughts of him did steal into her mind from time to time, but they weren't stressful thoughts. Not at all. How was it that in the middle of such a terrible situation she had found such happiness?

"Now what—or should I say who—put that smile on your face?" Carlotta, one of the med techs, teased as she deposited a stack of reports on Rebecca's desk.

Rebecca focused on the reports. "I was just daydreaming."

"Must be some daydream." Carlotta walked away, laughing.

Rebecca's lips curved in a smile once more. It had been a long time since she had been involved with anyone. She had forgotten how much fun new relationships could be.

She decided to eat lunch at her desk while she caught up on paperwork. With the front door locked and the phones forwarded to the answering service, she would have an hour and a half to make serious headway through the stack of papers and files. She had just set a cup of soup and a fresh mug of coffee beside her desk when her cell phone buzzed, indicating a new text message. Her heart jumped, and she fished the phone from her pocket, hoping the caller was Wes.

CASH. The name glowed bright at the top of the text.

I'm okay. Sorry to worry you. Have some things to deal with. Talk later.

Heart racing, she read the message through twice, then hit the call button. The phone rang twice before an electronic voice said, "You are being transferred to a voice mailbox."

"Cash! Cash! Pick up please. This is Aunt Rebecca. I got your message. Cash, please tell me what's going on."

She ended the call, then sent a text with the same message. She held the phone, staring at the screen, willing him to reply. But…nothing.

She jumped up and ran into Linda's office. "I have to go," she said. "I just heard from Cash and I need to tell the sheriff."

Linda stood and came around the desk. "Is he all right? Are you all right?"

Rebecca thrust the phone at her. "This is all he says. My call back went straight to voice mail and he hasn't answered my text. I need to let Wes know. Maybe they can trace the call or something and find him."

"Of course. Go. Tell them. And I'm glad he's all right."

Rebecca nodded and left the building. She didn't bother with her car but walked the few blocks to the sheriff's department, continually glancing at her phone, praying for a reply. But the phone remained still and silent.

She burst into the lobby of the sheriff's department. "I need to see Wes. Deputy Landry."

Adelaide Kinkaid rose from behind her desk. "Rebecca, what's wrong?"

"I heard from Cash. He says he's all right." She held out her phone. "I need to show this to Wes. Maybe they can trace the call."

"Deputy Landry is on a call right now…"

"It's okay, Adelaide." Wes moved toward them. Gently, he took the phone from Rebecca and slipped his arm around her. "Come into my office."

"I tried calling and texting, but he hasn't answered," she said. "But that's his phone number."

He sat her down, then took his seat across the desk from her and scrolled through the messages on her phone. She sat on the edge of the chair, tensed, until he finished making notes and laid the phone down.

"Can you trace it?" she asked. "Can you figure out where he is?"

"We can try," he said. "Do you have any ideas where he might be?"

She shook her head.

"Maybe he said something—an offhand remark that didn't connect for you until now."

She bit her lip, trying to come up with anything that would help. "He mentioned climbing in Grand Teton some day. But if he was going to do that, he wouldn't have left his truck and his climbing gear behind. And how did he get to wherever he is without his truck? Or most of his clothes?"

"It could have been an impulsive decision. He got a chance to go with someone else and did."

"Except that none of his friends are missing."

"Maybe it was someone he just met. Or someone he knew before, who was passing through the area."

"Then what was his truck doing wrecked at the bottom of that ravine?"

Wes leaned across the desk toward her. "I know there's not much to go on, but does that message sound like Cash to you? Are the words ones he would use?"

She frowned. "Yes. I mean, it doesn't *not* sound like him. Do you think it isn't him?"

"Anyone who found the phone and was able to unlock it could pull up the contacts and send a text like that."

"But they'd have to know how to unlock it. It's fingerprint technology, right?"

"There are ways to get around that."

She sat back, deflated. "Are you saying you don't think Cash sent that text?"

"We don't know. But it might not be."

She nodded, trying to let this sink in. After a moment, she said, "I can think of one reason he might have left town suddenly, without telling anyone. Maybe he was afraid. Maybe he knows who killed Basher and he's hiding from them. It would explain why he wrecked his truck. He pushed it into that ravine so that whoever was after him would think he's dead."

"Yes," Wes said. She could see on his face that he had considered this possibility also. He picked up the phone again. "We'll get to work trying to find a location this text was sent from."

"Have you found out any more about Bart Smith?" she asked.

"No, but we're working on it."

"Of course." She stood. "I should get back to work, too."

He stood also and moved around her toward the door, but instead of holding it open for her, he shut it firmly, then turned to her. "Come here," he said, reaching for her.

She moved into his arms and laid her head on his shoulder. This was what she needed right now. To be reminded that she wasn't in this alone. "I'll let you know as soon as I know something," he said.

That was enough. Not everything she wanted, but for now, it was enough.

Chapter Thirteen

Wes spent the rest of the afternoon working with Cash's cell phone provider to track down the location from which the text message to Rebecca had been sent. While he waited to hear back from them, he contacted the Colorado Springs Police Department. He was transferred to several people until he was finally forwarded to Detective Mike Paredo. "I remember Brad Monroe," Paredo said. "An educated kid from a good family who got sucked under by addiction. Too many of these kids end up dead before their life has really started."

"The tox report on Monroe came up clean for drugs," Wes said. "And there's no indication he's been using since he moved here a few months ago. But we're wondering if his death is linked to something that happened to him before. I understand the last time he was arrested in Colorado Springs he had agreed to testify against his supplier."

"And you think the supplier came after him as payback. It could happen."

"Who was the supplier?" Wes asked.

"Don't know," Paredo said. "We were counting on Monroe to tell us that, but he disappeared. What was he doing in Eagle Mountain?"

"Working odd jobs and rock climbing, living in an old ambulance he'd converted to a camper. Using his brother's ID and going by the nickname Basher."

"That sounds like he was hiding, all right," Paredo said. "From us, and maybe from his old drug connections, too. Maybe one of them did track him down. These people don't take kindly to anyone who cooperates with the law."

"Does the name Bart Smith ring any bells for you? I suspect it's an alias."

"No. How does this Smith figure into this?"

"We know that Monroe and a couple of other climbers met with a man by that name a couple of days before Monroe died. He had supposedly advertised for someone to do menial labor on a ranch he owned, but at the interview he brought up some extra unspecified work he'd be willing to pay more money for. He was wearing an obvious disguise—a fake wig—and was evasive enough that at least one of the young men suspected he was involved in something illegal, possibly drug trafficking."

"Huh. It sounds interesting, but I can't help you out."

"Have you heard of any players in the local drug scene who have moved out of the area?" Wes asked.

"No. But I'll do some looking around and let you

know if I hear of anything. Do you have new activity on your side of the state?"

"Not that I'm aware of, but maybe someone was getting ready to open up a new operation here. Maybe Monroe didn't recognize him because of the disguise, but he recognized Monroe and decided to shut him up before he put two and two together and got in the way."

"It's a good theory, but try proving it. These guys learn to cover their tracks pretty well."

"I worked Vice for twelve years in St. Louis," Wes said.

"Then you know. Good luck to you, Deputy. I'll let you know if I find out anything that might be useful."

At six o'clock, after consulting with Travis, Wes decided to bring Payson Fritsch in for questioning. Payson agreed to stop by the station *just to talk*, though when he arrived, he was fidgeting and pale. Most people were nervous around law enforcement, especially when a serious crime was involved. Wes didn't think the young man was guilty of anything, but he had a sense there was more Payson hadn't told them.

Wes led him to an interview room, where Travis joined them, and Wes went through the formalities of establishing time, place and who was there for the recording. Payson's eyes widened when Wes recited the Miranda warning. "I'm not in trouble, am I?" he asked. "I haven't done anything wrong."

"We just have some more questions for you," Wes said. "And we want to make sure we have everything on the official record. I'd like you to tell me everything that happened last Saturday, from your first encounter with Cash Whitlow and Basher Monroe to your last."

"Um, okay." He clasped his hands and rested them on the table in front of him. "So I go to Caspar Canyon where a bunch of us go to climb on Saturdays, about ten o'clock. Cash was there, and Basher. They were getting ready to climb this cliff face that kind of slants back over the water. A little challenging, but those two make it look easy. Cash was on the ground while Basher climbed, so I started talking to him, and I told him about this job I'd seen advertised—this guy looking for someone to work on his ranch. I've been looking for some part-time work and Cash knew that. I showed him the index card I took from the laundry bulletin board, with the guy's phone number."

"Why did you take the card from the bulletin board?" Wes asked.

"I didn't want anyone else seeing it and getting the job before I even had a chance."

"Do you still have the number? On your phone?"

"Uh, yeah. I guess so." He pulled his phone from his pocket and scrolled through. "I think it's this one," he said and handed over the phone.

Wes passed the phone to Travis, who wrote down the number and returned the phone to Payson. "All right," Wes said. "Go on with your story."

"So, I showed Cash the card and told him I had an interview with this guy, Bart Smith, in a couple of hours. Cash was pretty interested. He asked if he could come with me to talk to the guy." He fell silent, looking conflicted.

"Did it strike you as odd that Cash wanted to go along?" Wes asked.

"Well, yeah. I thought maybe he wanted to poach the job. And he's older than me and really outgoing and friendly. I figured Smith would want to hire him and not me. I told him I didn't think it looked good for me to bring a friend on a job interview. Like I was a kid or something." He wet his lips. "Could I have some water?"

"I'll get it." Travis left the room and Wes and Payson waited in silence until he returned with a bottle of water.

"Thanks," Payson said. He uncapped the bottle and drank half of it, then said, "Cash asked me where the ranch was and I said I didn't know—that Smith wanted me to meet him at the old gas station out on the highway.

"Then Basher finished his climb and came over and the three of us started talking. They asked me what I'd be doing at the ranch, and I said chores and stuff, but that Smith said I could earn extra money doing extra work. I thought that sounded pretty good, but Cash and Basher didn't like the sound of it. They said they thought they should come to the meeting with me.

"At first I said no again. But Cash said I needed to be careful. All this secrecy—Smith not wanting to tell me where the ranch was, meeting me at such an out of the way place and the offer to pay extra for extra work—but not saying what that work was—Cash said that might mean Smith was up to something illegal. Like drugs."

"Cash specifically mentioned drugs?" Wes asked.

"Yeah. And Basher said he thought the same thing. I felt pretty dumb for not having seen that before. So I said maybe I should call the whole thing off, and just not show. But Cash said no, we needed to know who this guy was, so we could warn other people. We'd bring Basher because he's a big guy and that would be good in case Smith got any ideas about taking advantage of me." He looked down at his thin arms. "I'm strong from climbing, but some people think I look pretty scrawny." He shrugged. "Anyway, they made it sound exciting. Like an undercover investigation or something. He and Basher were all up for it, so I went along with the idea."

"So what happened at the meeting? First, how did you get there?"

"Cash drove in his truck. We got there and at first it didn't look like anybody was there. Then this guy comes out from behind the station. We all kind of stared at first, because he looked like a joke. He had on this really fake black wig and a big straw cowboy hat and this Hawaiian print shirt with green alligators and pink flowers—it was just wild. But he acted like everything was normal. He walked up and shook our hands, introduced himself as Bart Smith. He didn't ask why Cash and Basher were there, just said he was glad to meet us.

"Cash and Basher let me do the talking. It went pretty much like a regular interview. Smith told me he was looking for someone to do manual labor on his ranch—clearing and burning brush, repairing fence, digging out rocks. He said he'd pay eight dollars an hour, which isn't bad for that kind of work, and I could set my own schedule, which was great. Then he said if I was interested, there'd be other work I could do for more pay. I asked him what kind of work and he said I'd have to wait until he was sure he could trust me before he told me more. I told him I'd think about it and let him know, we all shook hands again and then we got in Cash's truck and left."

"Where did you go?"

"Not far. I thought Cash was going to take me back to my car, but instead he drove down the highway a ways, then turned around and went back to the gas station. We were just in time to see a white SUV leaving the place. Cash said we should follow it and see where it went."

"Smith was driving the SUV?"

"I don't know. The windows were tinted and we couldn't really see the driver, but who else would it be, coming out of that abandoned gas station? And there was mud smeared all across the license plate, so you couldn't read it. Cash pointed that out and said it was clear Smith had a lot to hide."

"So you decided to follow the vehicle?"

"Cash decided. I was just along for the ride. I thought if this guy really was up to something illegal, he wasn't going to be very happy to have us following him. But Cash stayed pretty far back and the driver of the SUV never acted like he noticed us."

"Where did you end up?"

"We drove through town and out again, and the SUV turned onto County Road 361. Cash slowed way down, to put some more distance between us and the SUV, then he turned, too. But the guy must have turned off somewhere along the road pretty quick, because we drove up and down the road a couple of times and never did see the SUV again."

"Tell me more about the SUV. What kind was it?"

"I don't know. I mean, I'm not really into vehicles. It was just an SUV—a smaller one. White and kind of dirty. Like a lot of cars around here."

"What happened when you didn't find the SUV on County Road 361?" Wes asked.

"We came back to town and Cash dropped me off at my car. And that was it."

"You didn't hear anything from Cash or Basher again? No texts? Did you see them at all the rest of that day or Sunday?"

"No. I didn't think anything about it, until I heard that Basher was dead and Cash had disappeared." He leaned across the table toward Wes. "You don't think I'm in any danger, do you?"

"Has anyone threatened you?" Wes asked.

"No. Nothing like that. It's just kind of freaky that both of them are, well, gone now, and I'm still here."

"What did you think of Smith?" Travis asked. It was the first time he had spoken to Payson.

Payson shrugged. "I thought he was kind of a blowhard. I mean, it was hard to take anyone serious in that costume he was wearing, and it was an awful lot of drama for a job on a ranch. Why not just have me come to the ranch and talk about the job? If he did have some special *extra* work for me to do, why not wait until I'd worked for him a bit and we knew each other better before he offered it up? Why all the playacting?"

Why, indeed. "Thanks." Wes shook Payson's hand. "You've been a big help. If we have more questions, I'll be in touch."

"I can go now?" Payson stood.

"Yes. Thank you."

Wes walked Payson to the door, then returned to the interview room where Travis waited. "That number he has for Smith is a Colorado Springs exchange," Travis said.

"If Smith is up to something illegal, would he be dim enough to give out a number that could be traced?" Wes asked.

"Payson didn't think he was too bright."

"Yeah, but maybe that's part of the act. Doug Michelson at Colorado Mountain Guides said the man who came to his shop looking for Cash sounded like he was playacting, too."

"So, was that man—Bart Smith—the same man who killed Basher Monroe?" Travis asked. "And he planted the wig and the shirt in Basher's camper."

"Why? Cash and Payson know Smith and Basher aren't the same person because Basher came with them to the interview with Smith."

"He's already eliminated Basher, and maybe Cash, too," Travis said. "I'll have Shane do a few patrols in the area around Payson's place. He's on duty tonight."

"It's almost as if Smith is trying to draw attention to himself," Wes said. "But why? Because he wants to keep us from looking at something else?"

"Let's call his number and see who answers." Travis took out his cell and punched in the number.

"The number you have dialed is not a working number. Please hang up and try again."

Travis pocketed the phone again. "He ditched the number," he said.

Down the hall a phone rang. "Sounds like your phone," Travis said.

Wes hurried to answer. "Deputy Landry."

"Deputy, we traced the text you sent over to us," a woman's pleasant voice said. "It was placed from Colorado Springs. Downtown."

Colorado Springs. Basher was from Colorado Springs, and Bart Smith's no-longer-working number was a Colorado Springs exchange. What was the connection to Eagle Mountain?

Chapter Fourteen

Rebecca tried to stifle her disappointment when she didn't hear back from Wes all afternoon. She felt untethered without her phone, and more helpless than ever as she waited for other people to figure out where Wes might be. Questions played on an endless loop in her mind: Had Cash sent that message? Why would he have taken off the way he had? Was he in some kind of trouble?

It was after nine o'clock when someone knocked on her door, startling her. When she peered out the security peep, she was surprised to see Wes. She hurried to unlock the door and open it. "Hey there. I didn't see your car." She looked past him toward the curb, which was empty.

"I parked around back." He moved past her into the house, bringing the aroma of late summer: warm jasmine and pine.

"Why did you do that?" she asked.

"Because someone pointed out to me that if I'm going to spend so much time over here, I might want to be a little more…discrete." He pulled her close and kissed her, and the fierceness of her response to him still surprised her. She had never thought of herself as passionate, yet he brought out that side of her.

When they finally parted, he said, "Sorry I'm so late. There have been some developments. Nothing big," he hastened to add. "Just new information." He led her to the sofa and they sat.

"Did you find out anything about Cash's phone?" she asked.

"The text was sent from Colorado Springs."

"So… Cash's phone is in Colorado Springs?"

"Probably. Has he been there before? Does he have friends there he might have visited?"

"I don't think so. I think the only place in Colorado he's been is here. He drove here from California when he moved in, but I'm sure he didn't stop over in Colorado Springs. He's never talked about knowing anyone who lives there, though it's possible he knows climbers who have come here to climb. Maybe a client he guided?"

"What about his mom? Would she know?"

"I can call her and find out. But you still have my phone."

He took the phone from his pocket and handed it to her. "We're done with it now," he said.

She scrolled through her contacts and found Pamela's number, then glanced at the time. Only a little after eight o'clock at Pamela's house. "Hello, Rebecca," Pamela said. "You must be a mind reader. I was just thinking about calling you."

"Oh? Why is that?"

"I got a text from Cash this afternoon. As I expected, he decided to hare off somewhere and didn't bother to tell anyone. He says he's fine, not to worry." She laughed. "Didn't I tell you? It's so typical of him not to think about anyone but himself."

"Yes, he sent me a message, too." Rebecca met Wes's eyes. Should she say something about the possibility that the text hadn't come from Cash at all?

"Oh, good. When he decides to show up at your place again, you're welcome to read him the riot act on my behalf."

"Do you know if Cash has friends in Colorado Springs?" Rebecca asked. "Has he ever been there?"

"Why? Is that where you think he is?"

"I don't know. Someone mentioned it as a possibility."

"Huh. Well, I don't think he knows anyone there, but you know Cash. Maybe he met someone and they hit it off, and the next thing you know he decided to visit him. Or her." She sighed. "To be that young and carefree again."

"Let me know if you hear from him again," Rebecca said. "I'll do the same."

"Will do. You have a good evening."

She ended the call and Rebecca laid the phone on the coffee table. "Did you hear most of that?" she asked.

"I did. We've contacted police in Colorado Springs and we'll ask them to look for Cash."

"Why would he be in Colorado Springs? And without his truck and gear?"

"Basher Monroe was from Colorado Springs," Wes said. "Or at least he was there for a little over a year before he moved to Eagle Mountain."

"But Basher is dead. Why would Cash go there now?"

"I don't know. It's just a connection we're looking into. It might not mean anything."

"What about the search here?" she asked.

"Search and Rescue didn't find anything, and they did a thorough sweep of that ravine and the area above. We didn't find anything of particular interest in the truck, either."

"I want to go back out there and look for myself," she said. "I know I probably won't find anything, but I have to see for myself. I have to know I at least tried."

"Don't go by yourself," he said. "If you wait until Wednesday, I can go with you."

Waiting would be hard, but she didn't really want to conduct a search on her own. "All right," she said. "Is there anything I can do in the meantime?"

"Keep trying Cash's phone," he said. "And give yourself credit for already doing everything you can." He put his arm around her. "Patience is a lesson I have to learn over and over. It doesn't seem to get any easier."

"And we can't control other people." She sighed and leaned her head on his shoulder. "It's probably just as well we can't. I have enough trouble running my own life without having to be in charge of someone else's."

THE NEXT DAY, Wes returned to County Road 361. As he drove slowly down the gravel road, studying the landscape and the few residences, he wondered if Bart Smith lived or worked here, or if he had merely turned down this mostly deserted road because he realized he was being tailed and needed to evade his followers.

He decided to reinterview every person who lived on the road, and check for any white SUVs. He began at the end, with Martin Kramer. "I'm looking for a man who may go by the name of Bart Smith," Wes said. "Caucasian, six feet to six-four, broad shoulders and muscular." It wasn't much of a description. Thanks to the wig and sunglasses, they had no idea of Smith's hair or eye color.

"That description fits a lot of people," Kramer pointed out.

"Does anyone who lives around here fit that description?" Wes asked.

"I'm six feet tall," Kramer said. "And I'm strong enough."

This was true. Though Wes thought of Kramer as older—he was clearly in his sixties—he had an erect posture, and beneath the loose flannel shirt and baggy canvas work pants he wore was the hint of muscles. He would have to be strong to haul the buckets of rock that dotted the area around his shack.

"What's your phone number, Mr. Kramer?" Wes asked.

"There's no phone signal up here," Kramer said.

"Does that mean you don't have a phone? No means of communicating with the outside world?"

"I didn't say that. I've got a cell phone, but I don't even turn it on up here. It wouldn't do any good."

"What's the number?" Wes asked.

Kramer stuck out his lip, and Wes was sure he was going to refuse to answer the question, then he rattled off a number. Wes didn't recognize the exchange. "Where's that from?" he asked.

"Ohio. Where I used to live. And what's it matter to you?"

"Have you ever lived in Colorado Springs?"

"No. Why are you asking?"

"Just curious." Wes looked around the cluttered homestead, with its piles of old timber and many orange-and-white plastic buckets of rocks. No sign of any white SUVs, just a gray pickup. "Have you had any more trouble with trespassers?"

"No. I guess I scared them off."

"Let me know if anyone else bothers you."

Kramer turned away. "I have to get back to work now."

Wes moved on to the young couple in the yurt. Robby Olsen was mucking out the chicken house when Wes arrived, the stinging ammonia odor of the manure making Wes's eyes water. "Hello, Deputy," Robby said, wheeling a wheelbarrow full of bedding and manure out of the chicken run. "What can I do for you?"

Wes described Bart Smith. Becca Olsen walked over from the vegetable garden to join them. "Robby is six-two," she said and smiled at her husband.

Wes wouldn't have described Robby as broad-shouldered, but he was wiry, his arms corded with muscle as he propelled the full wheelbarrow forward. The young couple seemed innocent enough, but what better cover for illegal activity than a homestead in a remote area? "I'd really love a tour of your place," he said. "If you have time."

"Of course." Becca's smile was warm and open. "It's not fancy, but we're pretty proud of it."

Over the next half hour, Wes toured the yurt they called home, with its loft bedroom, woodstove, propane refrigerator and range, and solar-powered well. A separate washroom held a shower, laundry and composting toilet. He tromped past the chicken house, pigsty, goat barn, greenhouse and garden patch, a tool shed, wood shed and equipment storage. The Olsens drove a blue Volkswagen Jetta and a tan Chevy truck. They ended the tour back at Wes's cruiser.

"What are you really looking for, Deputy?" Robby asked, his tone not unfriendly. "You can see we don't have anything illegal around here."

"We received a tip that someone out this way was involved in illegal drug activity," Wes said. This wasn't entirely true, but close enough. "The tip was very vague—I don't know how credible it is, but I have to check it out."

"Of course," Becca said. She pressed her lips together and gave her husband a worried look.

"What are you thinking?" Wes asked.

"I hate to think anyone here is involved in that kind of thing," she said. "But the truth is we don't know our neighbors that well. Except for Lindsey and Micah Carstairs at the Russell Ranch. They're friendly, and I don't think they're involved in anything like that at all. But the couple in the trailer and Mr. Kramer—we just don't know them."

"Have you heard any more gunshots at Kramer's place?" Wes asked.

"Not lately," Robby said. "Things seem to have really calmed down. And Trey and Courtney keep to themselves and are pretty quiet. I don't think they're up to anything illegal, either." He frowned at his wife.

"I didn't say they were," Becca said. "Just that we don't know. And the one time I went over there to introduce myself and give them some vegetables from the garden, they made it pretty clear they didn't appreciate visitors." She shrugged. "I'm just used to people who are a little friendlier."

"Any increase in traffic on this road lately?" Wes asked.

They both shook their heads.

"Thanks. Let me know if you think of anything else that might be helpful."

"We will," Becca said. "But I hope your tip is wrong. We haven't had any trouble out here and we want it to stay that way."

Next stop was Trey Allerton's trailer. There was no sign of any vehicles parked there. Courtney Baker answered the door. She looked healthier today, with no bruises, her hair and makeup done. "What can I do for you, Deputy?" she asked. She wasn't smiling, but she wasn't hostile, either.

"Is Trey here?" Wes asked. Allerton, he knew, was the right build for Bart Smith, though, as he was quickly realizing, that didn't make him unique.

"He isn't," she said. "He went out of town on business for a few days, though I expect him back any time now."

"Where did he go?" Wes asked.

She hesitated, then said, "He went to Colorado Springs. He lived there before we moved here, and he still has friends there. But then you probably already know that."

It was probably in the file they had on Allerton, though Wes hadn't studied that. "What's his phone number?" Wes asked. "I just have a couple of questions. He could easily answer them over the phone."

She rattled off a number that was not the one for Bart Smith, but Wes made note of it. "One last question," he said. "What kind of vehicle does Trey drive?

"A Ford pickup. Why?"

"What color is it?"

"Black. What is this about?"

"Just filling in some blanks. Thank you for your help." He looked around. "Where is your car?"

"We don't need more than one vehicle, so we got rid of the other one."

"You're not worried about being stranded here by yourself?"

"I can always ask the neighbors if I need help."

"So you're all right here, by yourself?"

"I'm fine," she said. "I enjoy the peace and quiet."

"And your daughter—how is she?"

At the mention of her daughter, Courtney suddenly looked older, more drawn. "Ashlyn is with Trey. He thought the trip would make a nice treat for her."

"And you didn't go with them?"

She shook her head but didn't elaborate.

"But you're okay with her going with him?"

"Of course." She took a step back. "I have to go." Without waiting for a reply, she shut the door. He heard the lock turn.

He moved slowly away, his unease growing.

Back at the station, Jamie was at her desk. "I stopped by Trey Allerton's place this morning and talked to Courtney Baker," he told her. "She looks much better than the last time we saw her."

"That's good," Jamie said. "Maybe she really did fall down, but I think it's worth keeping an eye on her."

"I do, too. Allerton isn't home right now. She said he went to Colorado Springs for a few days."

"Maybe that's why she looks better." She shook her head.

"She told me they had sold her car, so with Trey

in Colorado Springs, she's there by herself with no transportation and no phone."

"That doesn't sound good," Jamie said.

"I asked her about it and she said she was fine, that she could ask the neighbors if she needed help," Wes said. "Which I guess is true, but it's still a long walk to any of her neighbors' houses. She also told me her daughter, Ashlyn, went to Colorado Springs with Trey."

"I really don't like the sound of that," Jamie said. "Who sends a three-year-old off with a man who isn't related to her?"

"Courtney says Allerton is like her stepfather."

"Still." Jamie shook her head. "I checked Allerton's file after we saw her last and there's nothing in there about inappropriate behavior with children. Not even a hint. But it still feels off to me."

"I think I'll contact the Colorado Springs PD again and ask them to do a welfare check," Wes said. "If they can find Allerton. I don't know where he's staying. But Courtney did give me his phone number. The police can start there."

And having the local police department contact Allerton would let him know he was being watched. Maybe it would make him less likely to step out of line. Or the Colorado Springs PD might catch him up to something illegal or find some evidence that tied him to Basher Monroe or Cash Whitlow. It was a long shot, but so much in solving crime came down to luck. Wes felt they were overdue for some luck when it came to this case.

Chapter Fifteen

Cash woke to light and cautiously sat up. His thigh, where the bullet had struck him, didn't hurt as much as it had, and he no longer felt feverish. But his stomach growled loudly. He had eaten the last beef jerky in his pack a long time ago. Day before yesterday? He had lost all track of time. But he needed to get out of here and find something to eat. And water. He was so thirsty. And he needed to let someone know where he was and that he needed help. If he could figure out how to get back to the road, maybe he could walk to a house, where someone would help him or at least let him use the phone to call Aunt Rebecca.

The ceiling in this cave was too low for him to stand upright. He had to walk hunched over to the entrance, then he had to inch along a narrow ledge before he reached a place where he could climb down a series of rock slabs. How had he ever made it up here, injured? He guessed he'd been desperate enough to do anything.

Once he was on fairly level ground, he tried to get

his bearings. He had no idea which direction he had come from that night. He'd simply been running, trying to get away from the old man who had shot at him and Basher. He had thought the old man wouldn't expect him to come back so soon, and alone. But he'd been wrong about that. Cash had been lucky to get away alive. He hoped the fact that the old guy had shot at him and at Basher, on two different occasions, would be enough proof that he must have something to hide for the sheriff's deputies to investigate. No way would someone be that protective of a bunch of worthless rocks.

Cash had intended to circle back to his truck and drive for help, but then the truck hadn't been where he'd parked it. What had happened? Had he gotten turned around and been wrong about the place he had left it? If he could find the truck, he could drive back to safety. But nothing about this area looked familiar. There was no road or even a trail to follow, just rocks and stunted trees.

His watch said he'd been away from home two weeks. Had it really been that long? He had been really out of it for a lot of that time and even now, walking out in the open, he was dizzy and unsteady on his feet. Maybe it had been more than a day or two since he'd eaten the last of the emergency supplies he'd had stashed in his pack. He really needed to get something to eat, and some water, before too much longer. How long did it take a person to starve to death or die of thirst? Did being shot shorten that time? He didn't know how much blood he had lost, though the side of his pants was stiff with it.

Don't think about dying, he told himself. He focused on walking downhill. After a while, he came to a stream and lay on his stomach beside it and drank and drank. He tried not to think about what might be in that water. He'd heard pretty much every body of water around here was contaminated with giardia, but he couldn't be picky right now. He sat up and pulled his water bottle out of his pack and filled it. He searched again for something to eat, but there wasn't anything. He'd taken all the ibuprofen from the first-aid kit, too. He wished he had his phone. He must have dropped it when he was running away from that miner.

His aunt Rebecca would be worried about him. Maybe by now she had even reported him missing. Which meant someone would be looking for him, but how would they know where to look? Rebecca had no idea where he had intended to go that day. Maybe Basher was feeling well enough now to talk to her.

He zipped up the pack, then froze. What was that noise, way off in the distance? It sounded like an engine. Maybe a Jeep or an ATV. That meant he was close to the trail. He pulled the pack onto his shoulders and stood, then closed his eyes and tried to zero in on the direction the sound was coming from. Then he set out walking.

He had almost given up on reaching the trail when he came upon it. He hadn't been able to hear the vehicle for a long time now, and figured it was a small miracle that he hadn't ended up walking in circles, the way lost people apparently did in the woods. He felt like crap, and kept stumbling over rocks or roots, but seeing the trail sent a surge of energy through him. He turned onto it and headed right—downhill. He would have run, but he didn't have the strength, so he settled on walking, eyes straining for some sign of civilization—a vehicle, a house, another person. Even a sign letting him know he was headed in the right direction would have been good.

He walked for what felt like at least an hour when the trail gradually began to widen. Soon the area began to look familiar. He stopped beside a wide, graveled area. The parking lot where he had left his truck. The lot was empty. Cash walked around it, staring at the gravel as if it might provide some clue as to what had happened to his truck. How did a whole truck simply disappear?

Finally he gave up and set off down the road. As he neared the Full Moon Mine, he moved off the road into the shelter of some trees, watching the driveway that led up to the old man's shack. The last thing he needed was the man with the gun seeing him out here. He'd probably decide to finish him off.

He stayed off the road until he could see the roof of a yurt ahead. He'd stop there and ask for help. But he didn't approach the yurt directly. Instead he crept up on it, hoping to get a feel for whether or not it would be safe. He didn't know these people. If they were the type to shoot trespassers, he wanted to know before they pulled out a gun.

An old tan pickup was parked on one side of the yurt, and some chickens scratched around in the dirt in a pen not far from the front door. But he didn't see any people.

There also weren't any no-trespassing signs or anything else to discourage visitors, so he decided to take a chance. He emerged from his hiding place behind a rock and walked up the driveway toward the front door. "Hello!" he shouted, in case someone was working in the barn or one of the sheds scattered around the place. But no one answered.

"Hello!" he called again.

Chickens clucked and scratched, and somewhere an animal—a goat or a sheep, maybe?—bleated. He leaned forward and tried to peer into the yurt. It looked deserted. He knocked again and tried the door. Locked. They probably had food in there, but he wasn't going to break in, even if he could figure out how.

He walked away from the yurt, toward the chickens. They probably laid eggs. Could he eat one raw? He decided he was hungry enough that he could do that, but only if he had to.

He moved past the chicken house to a plastic-covered greenhouse. The heat wrapped around him as he stepped through the door, along with the earthy scents of compost and greenery. Tomatoes shone red among the vines crowded along one side of the structure. Cash plucked one and bit into it like an apple, the juice running down his chin. He moaned—he had never tasted anything so good.

After the tomato, he picked a handful of green beans and ate them raw, along with a cucumber, some lettuce and another tomato. Not the most filling meal he had ever eaten, but it was food and it tasted good.

He thought about staying right here and waiting for the people who lived here to return. But how long would they be gone? What if it was several days? He decided he'd better move on.

The road was dusty, the sun glaring off it so bright he had to squint. His head throbbed and his leg ached, and despite the vegetables he had just eaten, or maybe because of them, his stomach hurt.

He couldn't think about all that. He had to keep going. He had to find help. The sound of tires on gravel made him freeze. He looked over his shoulder to see a vehicle approaching—fast, from the direction he had just come. Was it the old miner? Or someone else? He stepped to the side of the road, torn between hiding and asking for help. The vehicle was really moving now, rocks pinging off the undercarriage, dust rising in a huge cloud around it. Cash dove behind a clump of bushes as it roared past.

From here on the ground, he couldn't tell who was driving. He lay there for a long time, panting, but finally forced himself to his feet and kept going, staggering down the road.

He reached the driveway of the house trailer. There

were no cars out front, and the place looked deserted, but he limped up the steps and pounded on the door. No one answered. He pounded harder. "Help!" he shouted. "Somebody, please help!"

He pressed his ear to the door, listening, but heard nothing. He wanted to sink down to the steps and cry. Or maybe he should try to break in and find food and water. He tried the door, but it didn't budge and he didn't have the strength to kick it in or any tools to open it.

Defeated, he turned away and kept going. There was a ranch at the end of the road. Surely someone there would be able to help him.

He hadn't gone far before he heard another vehicle approaching. This time he didn't try to hide. If he lay down in the ditch again, he might not have the strength to get up. Instead he raised his hands in the air and waved.

The vehicle—a dirty white SUV—stopped in the middle of the road. The passenger window lowered and Cash limped over to it. A man with a big black mustache, a hat pulled low over his forehead, looked at him from behind dark sunglasses. "Please," Cash said, "I need help. Could I use your phone to call my aunt?"

"I don't have a phone," the man said. He sounded annoyed. But Cash couldn't worry about that. The man had stopped, so that was something.

"Then could you give me a ride into town?"

"What are you doing out here?" the man asked.

"My name is Cash Whitlow. My aunt Rebecca works at the medical clinic in town."

"I didn't ask who you are. I asked what you're doing."

Yeah. Not friendly. Well, he didn't have to be Cash's buddy. He just had to help him. "It's a long story, but a friend and I were…we were hiking…and this crazy old man started shooting at us. One of the bullets grazed me." He half turned and showed the tear in his jeans where he could feel the wound seeping something sticky and damp.

The man stared at him. "Get in," he said.

Cash didn't hesitate. He climbed into the passenger seat. "Thanks a bunch, mister," he said as the man shifted into Drive. "You can drop me off at the clinic right in town."

But instead of turning back toward town, the man kept going back the way Cash had come. "Uh, you can just take me to town?" Cash said.

The man didn't say anything.

"Where are we going?" Cash asked. He put one hand on the door release, then heard the lock click into place.

"I have something I need to do first," the man said. He glanced at Cash. "Don't worry."

Cash sat back and tried to remain calm. To think. He felt sick to his stomach, whether from fear or the pain in his side or from all those raw vegetables he'd eaten earlier, he didn't know.

The truck bumped along the road, every jolt sending fresh pain through Cash's body. The driver didn't look at him or say anything. His silence made Cash even more nervous. "Thanks for giving me a ride," Cash said. "What's your name?"

The man didn't answer. The guy was seriously creeping Cash out.

At the sign for the Full Moon Mine, the truck slowed. Cash held his breath, willing the driver not to turn in here. Were he and the old man with the gun working together? Had Cash chosen the exact wrong person to ask for help?

Then the SUV sped up again and they passed the driveway. "You said you were hiking with a friend," the driver said. "What happened to him?"

What should he say? He'd already lied about what they had been doing. "He was shot, too, but he managed to get away. I ended up lost."

"Some friend."

Cash wanted to protest that it hadn't been like that, but why bother? He couldn't really explain what he'd been up to, just in case the old miner and this guy were partners, or friends, or something.

"What were you really doing out here?" the man asked.

"I told you, we were hiking."

"I recognize a lie when I hear one. I bet you were snooping around. Poking your noses into something that's none of your business."

"What are you talking about?" Cash asked. "Why would I care about anything anyone out here is doing?" Unless they were doing something illegal. So was this guy partners with the old miner? Or did he have his own illegal activity he didn't want anyone to know about? "Where are we going?" he asked again. "The road stops up here just a little way."

"I know."

Cash was still trying to figure out what was going on when they reached the parking area. The driver turned in. "Get out," he said.

Cash got out. What else could he do?

By the time he'd eased out of the SUV and shouldered his pack, the driver was standing at the back bumper of the vehicle. Cash yelped when he realized the man was holding a pistol.

"The thing you need to realize—" the man said and raised the pistol "—is that we don't like trespassers around here."

Cash didn't wait for the man to fire. He turned and ran into the woods. Gunfire echoed loud behind him, but he kept running. Pain seared through him with every footfall, tears streaming down his face. He didn't want to die. Why were all these people trying to kill him?

Chapter Sixteen

Rebecca had asked for and received a half day off on Wednesday. "Is everything all right?" Linda asked when she made the request.

"Cash's truck was found in a ravine off the Jeep trail above County Road 361," Rebecca said. "I need… I need a couple of hours to take care of some things related to that." Some people might point out that it wasn't absolutely necessary for her to go back to the area where the truck had been found, to search for a young man who might very well be safe in Colorado Springs. But she needed to go for her own peace of mind.

"Oh, Rebecca." Linda's face filled with concern. "I'm so sorry."

"Thank you. They didn't find Cash with the truck, so I guess that's good. I'm still holding out hope."

"So am I." Linda leaned forward and squeezed her hand. "Do you need to go now? We'll manage, I'm sure."

"No. What I need to do can't be done until this afternoon." When Wes had time off as well.

She returned to her desk. As usual, the clinic was busy. They treated a boy who had fallen off his skateboard and broken his arm, and a woman with strep throat. Rebecca was entering some patient information when a bearded man in a dirty flannel shirt and canvas trousers walked up to the window. "I don't have an appointment, but I think I need stitches," he said. He held up his arm, wrapped in what looked like a dish towel, blood seeping through the fabric.

"Of course." Rebecca stood. "I'll get someone to see to you right away, Mr...?"

"Kramer. Martin Kramer. And no, I've never been here before. I don't get sick." He said the words as if health was merely a matter of refusing to give in to illness.

Rebecca summoned Gail, who took one look and escorted Mr. Kramer to an empty exam room. Rebecca followed, clipboard in hand. "While Gail is taking a look at your arm, I'll fill out the paperwork," she said. Not only did this allow her to get the information they needed without delay, talking to her would help distract the patient while Gail washed and assessed the wound.

She learned that Martin Kramer was sixty years old and had good health insurance through his former employer in Ohio. "What is your address, Mr. Kramer?"

He rattled off a PO box in town.

"What is your physical address?"

"I'm at the Full Moon Mine, 1162 County Road 361."

Rebecca stopped writing, her pen digging into the form. County Road 361. Near where Cash's truck had been found. This was the man Wes had told her about—the one who had complained of someone in a hoodie trying to steal from him. A young man who might have been Cash.

"How did you do this?" Gail asked. She had finished unwinding the towel to reveal a six-inch long cut seeping blood.

"I was transferring ore from one of the mine tunnels, loading it into buckets," Kramer said. "I reached into one of the buckets and cut my arm open on a big shard of glass."

"What kind of glass?" Gail asked. "A broken bottle?"

"This was more like window glass. A big, jagged piece." He shook his head. "I don't know where it came from or how it got into that bucket."

"You're lucky you didn't slit your wrist open."

He winced as she began cleaning the wound. "Do you know when your last tetanus vaccination was?" Gail asked.

"No."

"Then you'll need another one." She laid a gauze pad over the wound. "You hold that there—tight, please. Our nurse practitioner will be in in a moment to stitch you up. Rebecca will finish getting your information."

She left the room and Rebecca moved closer to

Kramer. She couldn't stay too long or someone might get suspicious, and she couldn't risk the nurse practitioner, Lauren Baker, overhearing what she had to say. "Mr. Kramer, my nephew, Cash Whitlow, is missing," she said. "His truck was found in a ravine off County Road 361. Not far from where you live."

"I've seen the posters about him. What's that got to do with me?"

"I was wondering if you had seen him. Or his truck. It's a gray Toyota Tacoma."

Kramer shook his head. "I'm too busy working to pay attention to whoever drives up and down my road. And if anybody comes on my property, I make it clear they need to leave."

Someone tapped on the door. "Mr. Kramer?" The door opened and Lauren moved in. "Oh, Rebecca. I didn't know you were still here."

"I was just leaving." She scooted past Lauren, out of the room. Kramer would need to sign the forms before he left, but that could wait.

She couldn't say why she felt so disappointed over the encounter. There was no reason Kramer should have had any contact with Cash, but so few people lived on that road she had hoped he might have some information that would link Cash with that area. An area where Cash really had no reason to be.

She returned to her desk and began entering Kramer's information into the computer. She was almost done when another man approached the check-in counter, this one more familiar. "Hello again," Trey

Allerton said. He flashed his movie-star smile and held up a flyer. "I hope you'll let me put one of these up on your bulletin board." He nodded to the board in the waiting room filled with announcements of local activities.

"What is it?" she asked and held out her hand.

"I'm going to be hosting a weeklong camp for local students next month," he said. "I'm trying to get the word out."

"What kind of camp?" The heading on the flyer was for Baker Youth Ranch. "You run a youth ranch?"

"We don't have permanent facilities yet, but we'll have tents, and plenty for the kids to do. And this will be at a very reasonable cost."

"I'll have to ask the clinic director," she said, setting the flyer aside. "If she okays it, we'll put it on the board."

"Be sure and let her know I'm accepting donations to underwrite the cost," he said. "Perhaps the doctors would like to contribute."

"I'll let them know."

"Any news about your nephew?"

She studied him. His expression was one of genuine concern, but she didn't trust this man. Then she remembered that he lived on Country Road 361. "The sheriff's department found Cash's truck in a ravine not far from where you live," she said. "A gray Toyota Tacoma. You didn't happen to see it driving around there, did you?"

"No. What would Cash have been doing out there?"

"I don't know. I think he and a friend might have driven out there to look for a man they knew. Someone named Bart Smith." She had almost forgotten about Smith. Why hadn't she asked Kramer about him?

Allerton's expression didn't change. "Never heard of him, and I know everybody on that road. Not that there are many people to know. Why were they looking for Smith?"

"I don't know."

"Young people are so impulsive," he said.

"What do you mean?"

"Just that it's not unusual for them to make sudden decisions. You know, let's take a road trip to the beach or let's climb this peak that hasn't been climbed before. I'll bet your nephew did something like that. He's probably on a beach a thousand miles from here, not even thinking about how he's worrying everyone."

"If that's so, how did his truck end up at the bottom of a ravine?"

Allerton shrugged. "Maybe his impulse wasn't to take a sudden vacation but to get involved with something he shouldn't have."

The hair on the back of her neck rose. His tone was still light and conversational, but the words chilled her. "What kind of thing do you mean?"

"I'm just speculating," he said. "I don't know anything. But maybe they found this Mr. Smith and he wasn't too happy that they had followed him."

"You're frightening me," she said.

"I don't mean to do that." He nodded toward the

flyer. "I'd appreciate you putting that out for me. Thanks."

He started to turn away when Martin Kramer, arm bandaged, was escorted out of the exam room by Gail. "She says I have to go to the hospital to get checked out for tendon damage," Kramer grumbled. "You've got to call over and let them know I'm coming."

"Mr. Kramer, what happened to you?" Allerton called.

Kramer scowled at Allerton. "None of your business."

"It looks like you hurt your arm," Allerton said. "You need to be careful, messing around in that mine."

"I don't need your advice," Kramer said. "I need people to leave me alone." He leaned across the counter toward Rebecca. "The more I think about it, the more I believe someone put that glass in that pile of rock. They knew I'd be moving that rock eventually and this was tucked in where it was hard to see, but could do a lot of damage. I'm lucky I didn't bleed to death out there."

Rebecca wasn't sure how to respond to this. She picked up the phone. "I'll call the hospital now." She leaned over and closed the window in Allerton's face. He was still staring at Kramer, his expression amused. "Mr. Kramer, do you know anyone named Bart Smith?" she asked while she waited for someone to answer her call.

He shook his head. "No. Who is he?"

"It's not important." Someone picked up at the hospital and she informed them the clinic was sending over a patient. She had just hung up the phone when the window slid open and Allerton leaned in again, as if he had been waiting for her to finish the call. "Kramer, do you want me to take you to the hospital?" he asked. "You probably shouldn't drive in your condition."

"I drove all the way here, didn't I?" Kramer barked. "I don't need your help."

"I'm just trying to be neighborly."

Kramer mumbled something under his breath that wasn't very complimentary to Allerton. "Thank you, Mr. Allerton," Rebecca said. "I think Mr. Kramer will be okay." She closed the window again.

Kramer signed the forms she slid toward him. "Everything out my way was nice and quiet until he moved in." Kramer jerked his head toward the window. Allerton was gone, but Rebecca understood his meaning.

"Is Mr. Allerton not a good neighbor?" she asked.

"He doesn't know how to mind his own business. He's always stopping by to check on me. But I know he really just wants to nose around, see what I'm up to. And he's always going on about this youth camp he's going to operate. Not about the kids he wants to help so much, but about how expensive it is to build a project like that, and don't I want to make a donation? He's one of those people who always has their hand out, but once they get money from you, all they want is more. He's hit up everybody in the county and must have collected a dump truck load of cash by now, but he hasn't done one thing to that worthless piece of land he leased from Sam Russell that I can see. Well I can tell you one thing—he'll never get a dime out of me, no matter how hard he tries."

He left, and Rebecca returned to entering his information into the computer. But her encounter with Allerton had shaken her. Had Cash and Basher found Bart Smith? Had Smith killed Basher? Was Cash dead, too?

The thought made her feel hollow and cold. She had meant it when she told Linda she wasn't giving up hope. But the longer Cash remained missing, the harder it was to believe he was all right.

"WE TRACKED ALLERTON to a motel on the north side of town where he was staying, but he checked out yesterday," Detective Paredo with the Colorado Springs Police Department said.

Wes cradled the phone against his shoulder and made a note of the name of the motel. "Any luck locating Bart Smith?" he asked.

"He's not in our records, none of the motels I talked to while looking for Allerton had heard of him, and no one I talked to knows anyone by that name. Of course, it could be a new alias."

"What about Allerton? Is he in your records?"

"He's never been charged with anything. His name came up in connection with a couple of things—an assault and a fraud case—while he was stationed at

Fort Carson. But only peripherally. He knew the people involved—that kind of thing."

That fit with the pattern Allerton had shown here of associating with the wrong people.

"What about Martin Kramer?" Wes asked. "Does that name ring a bell?"

"No. Who's Kramer?"

"He has a gold mine up here. A neighbor of Allerton's."

"I'll run a search on him for you, but I've never heard of him. I did check out your missing person— Cash Whitlow. We don't have anything on him, either. A dead end on the phone, too."

"Yeah, the phone company told me no more calls or texts are being sent from that number. No signal, either."

"Whoever had it probably destroyed it," Paredo said.

"Maybe so."

"Sorry I couldn't be of more help," Paredo said.

Wes hung up the phone and looked up at Gage, who had walked over to lean against his desk. "We should ask Trey what he was doing in Colorado Springs," Gage said.

"He'll say he was visiting friends."

"Or raising money for his youth camp. That's his full-time occupation these days." Gage stretched, cracking his knuckles. "I'd love to take a look at his bank accounts, figure out where all that money is going."

Wes wasn't interested in Trey Allerton. Not unless he could be tied to Basher Monroe's murder or Cash Whitlow's disappearance. "Have you had any luck tracking down Bart Smith?" he asked.

Gage shook his head. "I talked to every landlord in town, and every retail business. Nobody knows him. No business made a credit card sale to that name and no one rented lodgings to him."

"I'm convinced Bart Smith isn't his real name," Wes said.

"There's another possibility," Gage said.

"Oh?"

"Maybe Payson Fritsch made up the whole story."

Wes nodded. That kind of thing happened all the time. "Did Payson strike you as the typical attention seeker, though?"

Gage shrugged. "Maybe it started out as a joke between the three of them."

"If that's so, it's a joke that got way out of hand, considering Basher is dead."

"Speaking of that, we got forensics back on the bullets that were in Basher. Just like Doc Collins said— a 12-gauge slug and 45 ACP. Common loads. Martin Kramer bought some of each at the hardware store here in town, but—and this is interesting—Trey Allerton purchased a box of 45 ACP a couple of weeks ago."

Allerton again. What was with the guy? Wes stood. "I'm taking Rebecca back out to the area where Cash's truck was found," he said. "I doubt we'll find anything, but she insisted on taking another look and I wasn't about to let her wander around out there by herself."

"Good idea," Gage said.

The two of them walked together to the lobby, where Adelaide appeared to be arguing with a familiar figure. "Trey, what are you doing here?" Gage asked.

Trey Allerton's expression brightened when he saw them. "Deputy Landry," he said. "Courtney told me you stopped by to see her yesterday."

"She said you were in Colorado Springs," Wes said. "Did you have a good trip?"

"I did." He held out a single sheet of paper. "I want to put this poster in your window."

"I've tried to explain to Mr. Allerton that we don't allow businesses to advertise on sheriff's department property," Adelaide said.

"It's not exactly a business," Allerton said. "It's a benefit to the community—a weeklong camp for local youth."

"Which you are charging for," Adelaide said.

"A very reasonable fee. And I'm asking local businesses and organizations to donate to underwrite the expense, if the sheriff's department would like to contribute."

"I didn't think you had any facilities to host campers yet," Gage said.

"This will be in tents," Allerton said. "It's a good way to publicize what we're doing, get locals familiar with the project and invested in it. This kind of thing can be good for the whole town."

"How's the fundraising coming?" Gage asked.

"It's a process. Would you like to make a personal donation? We can always use funds."

"Not right now," Gage said.

Wes returned the flyer. "Better find someplace else to hang this."

Adelaide sniffed and returned to her desk.

Allerton opened his mouth as if to protest, but Wes cut him off. "I'm glad you stopped by. I wanted to ask if you knew Basher Monroe."

"The young man who was killed? I read the story in the paper. But no, I didn't know him."

"I thought you might have," Wes said. "He used to live in Colorado Springs, too."

Allerton shook his head. "I didn't know him. But that's not surprising, really. I was in the military at the time. I didn't interact much with the locals."

According to Detective Paredo, that wasn't true, but Wes didn't contradict him.

"How's the search for Cash Whitlow coming?" Allerton asked. "I stopped by the clinic just now and his aunt Rebecca told me you found his truck not far from where I live."

"We did," Wes said. "Do you have any idea how it might have ended up there?"

"Rebecca said he and a friend were out there looking for someone they knew."

"Bart Smith. Do you know him?"

"No. It sounds like a fake name, doesn't it? Initials B.S." He chuckled.

"Fake or not, Bart Smith may have murdered one young man and be involved in the disappearance of another," Wes said. "If you know anything that could help us find him or Cash Whitlow, you need to tell us."

"All I know is what I told Rebecca. Young men can be impulsive. Maybe Cash and his friend got involved in something that wasn't their business."

"Such as?" Gage asked.

"I wouldn't know," Trey said. "But it doesn't take a genius to figure out that it would be relatively easy to hide all kinds of illegal activities in these remote areas. I mean, look at my neighbor, Martin Kramer. Do you have any idea what he's really up to in that mine of his?"

Had Allerton changed subjects in order to divert attention? "Do you think Mr. Kramer is involved in something illegal?" Wes asked.

"He just seems overly protective of his property to me. And if there's really gold in these old mines, why isn't everyone out digging it up? I think the mine would make a great cover for other kinds of businesses—drugs or smuggling or something."

"It sounds like you've given this a lot of thought," Wes said.

"It's pretty natural to wonder about your neighbors isn't it? Especially when one of them threatens you with a shotgun every time you pull up in the driveway."

"Maybe you need to stop visiting him," Gage said.

"Except maybe he's just a lonely old man in the

early stages of dementia," Allerton said. "If that's the case, I feel I have an obligation to check in on him." He waved the flyer. "I'd better get going. I want to post as many of these as possible."

"Thanks for stopping by," Wes said.

"Not at all," Allerton said. "Oh, and Deputy?"

"Yes?"

"You might want to have a talk with Rebecca Whitlow. When I spoke with her today, she asked a lot of questions about her nephew. She seemed to think I knew something. I'd hate for her to go snooping around the neighborhood, thinking she was helping her nephew, only to end up in trouble herself. I mean, she's a really nice lady, but probably a little naive about how dangerous some people can be."

"Do you have any particular dangerous person in mind?" Wes asked.

Allerton's expression remained guileless. "No one in particular, but she really needs to be careful."

Gage waited until Allerton had exited before he said, "Nice of him to be so *concerned* about his neighbor and about Rebecca."

Right. That hadn't sounded like concern to Wes. It had sounded like a threat.

Chapter Seventeen

Rebecca was waiting out front when Wes arrived to pick her up. "How are you doing?" he asked as she climbed into the front seat of the sheriff's department SUV.

"I don't know," she admitted. "I'm excited to be doing something other than sitting around worrying, but I know, realistically, that we probably won't find anything. And a couple of things happened at work this morning that are a little, well, unsettling."

"Oh?" Though his eyes remained on the road as he drove, she sensed that he was focused on her. "What happened?"

"Martin Kramer came in to the clinic. He's the miner you were telling me about, isn't he? He lives on Country Road 361."

"Yes. Why was Kramer at the clinic? Or are you allowed to say?"

"I can't imagine you'd have reason to tell anyone else. He cut himself on a piece of window glass. Lauren, our nurse practitioner, sent him to the hospital to make sure he didn't have tendon damage."

"Was he repairing a broken window or something? He made a complaint last week about someone trying to break in at his place."

"He said the glass was in a pile of rock he was transferring into five-gallon buckets. It was a pretty bad cut. He could have sliced an artery and bled to death."

"That seems a strange place for a piece of glass. Did he say how it got there?"

"He told me he thinks someone may have put the glass there, intending to hurt him. I thought maybe he was being paranoid. He'd already talked about warning off anyone who came to his place."

"He is paranoid," Wes said. "But sometimes people feel that way because they really are being persecuted."

"I asked him about Cash, and about Bart Smith, but he said he didn't know anything about them. How could all three of them have been out there and nobody saw them? There aren't that many people who live out there."

"Kramer is something of a hermit," Wes said. "I don't think he engages with a lot of other people if he can help it."

"Yes, that's the impression I got. He told me how much he doesn't like his neighbor Trey Allerton."

Wes glanced at her. "He specifically mentioned Allerton?"

"I think that was just because Allerton was at the clinic this morning, too. He dropped off a flyer about a kids' camp he's hosting. He didn't know Bart Smith, either, and he said Cash was probably off on a beach somewhere, oblivious to how worried I've been."

Wes nodded. "Allerton brought his flyer by the sheriff's department, too."

"Did he ask you for a donation?" she asked.

"I think he asks everyone for a donation."

"Kramer says he thinks all the money he collects goes into Allerton's pocket."

"He hasn't spent much on this so-called kids' ranch of his," Wes said. "But maybe he needs a lot of money before he can really start work. I don't have any idea what's involved in a project that size. For now, he says he's going to put the kids in tents."

"I wouldn't trust my kids to someone with no experience, no infrastructure and I'm assuming no staff— would you?"

"No. But a lot of people find Allerton very charming."

Trey Allerton was good-looking. And he exuded a kind of charisma. But she had always been leery of people who found it so easy to mesmerize others. "Do you think he's right?" she asked. "Do you think Cash is relaxing on a beach somewhere—or in Colorado Springs?"

"The police in Colorado Springs are looking for him, but so far they haven't found him," Wes said. "If he's staying with friends and staying out of trouble, there's no reason they should know he's there."

"I keep calling his phone, but I never get an answer."

Wes's jaw tightened, but he didn't say anything. He turned onto County Road 361 and she sat forward, studying the landscape as they passed. She wasn't sure what she was looking for, but she couldn't shake the belief that the clue to what had happened to Cash was somewhere on this road.

A young woman, belly round in the late stages of pregnancy, was walking back from her mailbox at the entrance to the Russell Ranch. She waved as they passed. "That's Lindsey Carstairs," Wes said. "She and her husband, Micah, are leasing the ranch. They both grew up in the area and have good reputations. I spoke to them about Cash and Basher, and about Bart Smith, but they didn't know anything."

"Everyone says they don't know anything," she said. "But someone has to know, don't they?"

"That's how a lot of criminal cases are solved," Wes said. "Someone who knows something comes forward. The key is finding that someone."

"Which is why I'm here today," she said. "I want to find that someone."

Wes slowed as they neared Trey Allerton's trailer. Allerton stood outside his door, watching as they passed. Wes lifted his hand in a wave, but Allerton didn't return the gesture. "I guess he's not feeling very charming today," Rebecca said.

"He thinks the sheriff's office is harassing him," Wes said. "He's been on the periphery of several of our cases, so he's been questioned a number of times."

"But he hasn't done anything wrong?"

"He hasn't been charged with any crime," Wes said.

"That's a very diplomatic answer."

He laughed, and her mood lifted at the sound. He drove past the yurt. "We've questioned the Olsens, too," he said. "They seem sincere in their desire to help, but they didn't have anything to tell us."

"When I think about it, I don't pay attention to every vehicle that drives down my street," she said. "And I don't know all my neighbors, though I do know most of them. They've been in the clinic at one time or another. But if someone wanted to keep to themselves, I probably wouldn't notice."

"Most people are too involved in their own lives to notice what's going on with others," Wes said. "It's not a bad way to live, though it makes investigations more difficult. There's nothing we like better than finding the nosy neighbor who knows what everyone else is up to."

"Too bad you don't have someone like that here."

The sign for the Full Moon Mine loomed ahead. "I'm tempted to stop by and see if Mr. Kramer is all right," she said. "Even though he complained about Allerton doing the same. He said Trey was just snooping. I can always claim a professional interest." He slowed as they neared Kramer's driveway. "Let's stop and talk to him a minute."

The SUV bumped and rattled up the driveway and came to a stop a hundred yards from a shack constructed of rough sawn lumber and sheets of corrugated metal. Wes waited a moment, then honked the horn. "When I was here before, Kramer didn't waste any time warning us off," he said.

"I don't see a vehicle," she said. "Maybe he's not back from the hospital yet."

"I'll just check around." He unfastened his seat belt and reached for the door handle. "Let me get out first, and make sure the coast is clear."

He opened the door and slowly eased out of the vehicle, then stood beside the SUV, looking around. He walked up to the shack and knocked. "Mr. Kramer! It's Deputy Landry. Are you all right?"

Rebecca could stand it no longer. She got out of the vehicle and hurried toward him. "I don't think he's here," she said.

Wes tried the door, but it didn't budge. "I think you're right." He nodded to their right. "Let's make sure he's not up at the mine."

A narrow gravel path led up the hill from the shack. Rebecca followed, and they picked their way around several orange plastic buckets of rocks, an overturned wheelbarrow and various rusted pieces of what she guessed was old mining equipment. At last they reached a rough timber shed over the dark hole in the side of the mountain. A sign proclaimed this to be Adit #1, Full Moon Mine. Estab. 2016.

Wes cupped his hands to his mouth. "Mr. Kramer!"

Silence enveloped them, so complete she might have believed she had suddenly lost her hearing, except she could make out the soft sigh of her own breath and the click of rock against rock as Wes shifted his feet. He knelt and touched something on the ground. "Blood," he said. "There's a trail of it back toward his shack."

How had Rebecca not noticed the bloodstains on their walk up the path? Now they seemed obvious—dark splotches in the gray gravel. But she had been looking for a complete man, not his blood. "It was a bad cut," she said. "He was smart enough to bandage it up tightly—not so easy to do for one person alone."

"I'm going to take a look inside." He took a flashlight from his utility belt and switched it on.

Rebecca followed him into the mine tunnel. Though she could remain upright in the narrow passage, Wes had to stoop. Kramer would have had to do so also. About twenty yards inside, the passage opened into a kind of room, a large pile of fist-sized rocks on either side. "This is where he cut himself," Wes said and played the beam of light over a larger bloodstain. Then he shifted the light to a piece of glass, about the size of a sheet of paper torn from a notebook. He knelt and looked at it more closely, then handed Rebecca the light. "Hold this so I can take a closer look," he said.

She did as he asked and he pulled a pair of thin gloves from his pocket and put them on. Then he picked up the glass by one corner and held it up. It glinted in the light, and she thought she could make out the thin stain of blood across one corner. "This isn't ordinary window glass," he said.

"It isn't?" That's exactly what it looked like to her.

"Look at this edge." He pointed to the longest edge. "I'm not positive, but it looks to me as if it's been filed, so that the edge tapers." He gingerly touched the edge. "It's razor sharp."

"Could it have broken that way?"

"I don't see how." He held the glass in one hand and fished in his pocket with another and took out a thick plastic bag. He deposited the glass in this, then took out a pen and wrote on the label on the bag. "I think I'll have the lab take a closer look at this," he said.

"Do you think Mr. Kramer is right?" she asked. "Someone deliberately planted that here?"

"I want to find out." He stood and took the flashlight from her, and shone it around the room. "Kramer has been working here five years. It's hard work. Why would he keep doing it if it didn't pay off?"

"Maybe he keeps going because he's convinced he'll strike it rich someday," she said. "Isn't that what keeps gamblers placing bet after bet, even after they've lost almost everything?"

"Maybe," Wes said. "Or maybe Kramer really has found gold and someone else knows it and is trying to steal from him."

They returned to the SUV, and Wes locked the glass in its evidence bag in a box in the back of the vehicle. Then he turned around and they headed back to the county road, and up the hill to the point where the road narrowed. A sign announced that only high-clearance, narrow wheelbase, four-wheel drive vehicles were allowed past that point.

Wes swung the SUV into the parking area to the left. Rebecca stared at the empty gravel lot. It looked familiar, yet also foreign. With the trees closing in around them and no more houses or driveways for reference, it was easy to lose track of where you were. "How far are we from where Cash's truck was found?" she asked.

"It's right below here." He got out of the SUV and she followed him to the edge. Bright yellow paint on the ground marked a pair of ruts from a vehicle. "This is where the truck went over," Wes said.

She stared at the faint impressions in the dirt and gravel and tried to imagine what had happened. "The parking area stops ten feet from the edge," she said. "How did Cash's truck get from there to here? Did he just drive? Maybe he didn't see the edge in the dark or thought he was farther away?"

"Maybe." He took her arm and led her away from the tracks. "But the forensics team think the truck might have been pushed over."

His grip on her arm tightened. "But we don't think Cash was in the truck when it went over," he reminded her.

"Then where was he?" The question came out as a wail, and she struggled to regain her composure. "None of this makes sense to me," she said.

"It doesn't make sense to me, either. Let's walk a little way up the trail and see what else we can see."

He didn't let go of her arm, and she didn't try to pull away. The warmth of his hand and the strength of his grip steadied her. She didn't have to go through any of this alone.

The trail itself was a rutted red dirt path, approximately four feet wide, stunted juniper trees and large boulders scattered on either side. The air at this elevation was cool and crystal clear, smelling of warmed granite and cedar, like an expensive men's cologne.

Wes studied the ground as they walked, slowly, down the middle of the road. "What are you looking for?" she asked.

"I'm not sure," he said. "Anything odd or different."

Like bloodstains, she thought, but didn't say so out loud.

Wes put up his hand, a signal for her to stop. Then he knelt and stared at the ground. Without changing her position, she tried to see what he was looking at. "Is that a footprint?" she asked.

"Part of one." He indicated what she could now see was the impression of the front half of a tennis shoe. "Someone stumbled and fell," Wes continued. He pointed to a rounded impression two feet ahead of the partial shoe print. "Here's his knee where he caught himself." He leaned forward, and so did she, her heart starting to beat faster when she saw the next clue. "And here's where his hand went down." He took out his phone and focused it on the spot. "I don't know how clear a photo I'll get in this dappled light, but it's such a clear impression, we might even be able to get fingerprints off of it. We'll definitely want to get a forensics team up here to make an impression."

The shutter of the camera clicked, a tiny sound in the vast empty space, and then sound exploded around them. Shards of rock flew up from the ground inches from where Wes knelt. A scream tore from Rebecca's throat and then Wes was shoving her to the ground. She flattened herself to the rough dirt, Wes's weight heavy on top of her, as another shot hit close to them. And another still.

Chapter Eighteen

Wes grappled to free his pistol from its holster, even as he tried to keep his body over Rebecca's. She lay still beneath him, unmoving except for the involuntary shudders that coursed through her every few seconds. She was shaking with fear. He might have done the same, but he didn't have time to be afraid. He was too busy processing everything that was going on. The shots were coming from behind them, back toward the parking area. Had someone followed them here? How had he failed to notice them, if that was the case?

He freed the weapon at last, and scanned their surroundings for the best place to shelter. He flattened his body over Rebecca again, and pressed his lips to her ear. "On the count of three, I'm going to roll off of you and I want you to drag yourself over behind that boulder," he said. "Do you see it, just ahead?"

"Yes," she whispered.

"Good. Are you ready?"

"Where are you going to be?" she asked.

"Right behind you."

"All right. I'm ready."

The shooter had stopped firing for the moment. But that might only mean he was moving closer, into a better position to finish them off. "One," Wes said. "Two. Three."

He levered himself off her and she dragged herself forward, scrambling on her knees. Another shot rang out and she stifled a cry but kept going. Wes didn't bother answering the fire. He had already assessed that their assailant was using a semiautomatic rifle. One with much greater range than Wes's Glock.

He followed her and they crouched behind the boulder. "Are you all right?" he asked.

"I'm terrified. But I'm not hurt." She sat on the ground, her back to the stone, while he leaned over her, staring in the direction he thought the shots had come from, but seeing nothing. Everything around them was utterly still and silent. "Who's shooting at us?" she asked.

"I don't know." Was it Kramer? Maybe he had seen them at his place and followed them here, though so far he had shown an inclination to fire only on people he deemed trespassers, and then his weapon of choice was a shotgun. It could be Bart Smith. Or someone else entirely.

Wes leaned around the boulder, and immediately another shot sent him diving for cover. Rebecca gripped his arm. "Don't do that!" she said.

He nodded but didn't answer, willing his heart to slow.

"What are we going to do?" she asked. "He has us pinned here."

He tried his shoulder-mounted radio, but raised only static. He might have better luck on the unit in the SUV. Though the police radio, like cell phones, didn't always work in these remote locations, a series of repeaters placed on peaks around the county had improved service of late. If they could get to the SUV, they would radio for help or even drive away.

"Let's see if we can move parallel to the road, back toward where we're parked," he said. He pointed behind them. "There, in that thick brush. If we can get on the other side of that, it will provide more cover."

She nodded. "Go now," he urged, and she darted forward, keeping low. No shots came. Had the shooter not seen her or was he taking advantage of their inattention to move even closer?

Wes followed Rebecca, and held back a tangle of branches while she wriggled her way in and through a tangle of vines. From here, they were able to keep a screen of shrubs, stubby trees, downed logs and other forest debris between them and the roadway. Wes worried the shooter was tracking them through the sounds of their movements. Dried leaves crackled and twigs popped underfoot, no matter how stealthily they tried to move.

They stopped when they were in sight of the SUV. It sat, undisturbed, where they had left it, but getting to it would require crossing the open roadway and the barren gravel parking area. "How are we going to get there without being shot?" she whispered.

"Let's wait a minute and see what happens." He strained his ears for any sign of movement around them.

"Maybe—" But he never heard what else she had to say. The back windshield of the SUV shattered as another shot echoed, this one sounding much closer to them. Two more shots shredded the back tires. So much for that avenue of escape.

The shooter knew exactly where they were, and he was coming closer.

Rebecca stared at Wes, wide-eyed, her fist over her mouth, as if stifling a scream. "We have to get out of here," he said. He pointed back the way they had come. "We'll run. Stay in cover if you can, but moving quickly is even more important. Zigzag from side to side and stay low to make yourself a smaller target. And don't stop. We need to put as much distance as we can between ourselves and whoever is shooting at us."

She lowered her hand and nodded. "All right."

"You go first." He wanted to put himself between her and the shooter. "I'll follow."

She frowned, but he didn't wait for her to debate him. "Go," he said and nudged her.

She went. Together, they crashed through the woods on a zigzagging course. The shooter fired after them, but they kept going, darting between trees. He spotted a narrow trail into deeper undergrowth and tugged her arm, indicating they should take it, and she veered onto it, ducking beneath a curtain of vines, around a fallen ponderosa pine and up a slope carpeted with moss.

His lungs burned and his side ached by the time she stopped in the shelter of a rock outcropping. She leaned against the rock and pressed her head to the rough surface, eyes closed, panting. He pressed his back to the same rock and stared up at a triangle of darkening sky showing through the canopy of leaves. "I haven't heard any more shots in a while," he said.

"Do you think he followed us?"

They would have been easy to track. They weren't trying to hide their path. But he had no sense that they were being pursued. "I don't think so," he said after a moment.

She hugged her arms around her shoulder. "It's getting colder," she said.

Even in summer, nights at this elevation held a chill. They needed to find shelter. He had emergency gear in the SUV. If they could make their way back to it, maybe they could get help at the yurt or at Russell Ranch. He trusted the Olsens and the Carstairs enough to go to them.

Rebecca straightened and brushed her hair back off her forehead. "Which direction do we go from here?"

He stood up straight also and looked back the way they had come. Or the way he thought they had come. Though he had felt as if they were bulldozing through the woods, on a path anyone could follow, he realized with a start that he could make out no sign of their passage. It was as if the forest had closed over their tracks.

"Wes?" she asked.

He took her hand and squeezed it. "I don't know where we are," he said. On top of everything else, they were lost.

CASH HEARD THE gunshots from his hiding place, under a rock overhang on the side of a hill. He hadn't been able to make his way back to the cave he had used before, but had found this sheltering overhang just before dusk. He woke from a fitful sleep, shaking with the visceral memory of the old miner firing at him and Basher, of Basher going down and the nightmarish hike back to the truck.

And then the next day, when he had come back to the mine and been shot himself. He had thought it was the miner wanting to finish him off, but now he wasn't so sure. The man in the white SUV who had driven him back to the parking area. Had that been Bart Smith? Or someone who was working for the old miner? Or someone else who simply wanted Cash dead?

He had run until he had fallen, too exhausted to get up, but he had made himself get up and dragged himself to this shelter. He didn't know how long he had lain here. The place where he had been shot was oozing blood and pus now, and his fever raged.

Was he going to die? When he was climbing, he never thought about death. Clinging to a rock face in the most precarious position, he always felt incredibly alive. But now, alone in these woods, hurting and hungry, death haunted him.

The shots sounded far away. Was it hunters, after a deer or the man with the big mustache? Was it the miner?

He struggled to sit up. Were the shots getting closer? He couldn't tell. He should move to a better hiding place. But where? And he couldn't keep hiding like this. When he had first retreated here, he had told himself that by now Aunt Rebecca would have reported him missing. People would be looking for him. All he had to do was wait for them to find him.

But what if they weren't looking? He couldn't stay here much longer, without food and water, waiting.

He forced himself to a standing position, though he had to hold onto the wall of the overhang to keep from falling over. Though he was some ways up the hill, he couldn't see much from here, except the tops of trees. Sometimes he could see deer moving through the woods below, and once he had watched a porcupine undulating its way up the trail, its lush cape of quills quivering with each step.

Then he saw the people—the woman first, then the man behind her. Was he following her? Was this the shooter?

But no. She stopped and waited for the man, then they embraced. They were together. A couple. Out hiking? He opened his mouth to shout, then remembered the shooter. He was still out there. If Cash drew his attention, would he kill these strangers, too?

Instead, he waited, watching. They were headed this way. When they were near enough for him to speak to them without shouting, he would do so. He'd warn them about the shooter. Though, surely, they would have heard the shots.

The man had dark hair, and was clean-shaven, so he wasn't the man who had given Cash a ride. And he wasn't the old miner. This man was younger.

He focused on the woman again. Something about her was familiar, but he only caught glimpses of her as she moved between the trees.

How long since the shooting had stopped? Since before he saw the man and woman? He felt as if he were trying to move through fog, drifting in and out of awareness, unable to keep track of time. He forced himself to focus on the man and woman again. They were definitely getting closer.

He was getting dizzy, standing so long, so he sat and watched the couple move up the slope toward him. He could only see the tops of their heads now. And the man's hand. He carried a gun. Had he been the one shooting?

Cash drew back. Maybe he should go back under the overhang and hide. Let these people pass.

But the woman was with this man. No woman had been with Bart Smith or the miner or the man with the mustache. And she didn't have a gun that he could see.

They were directly below him now, on the same path he had followed to this place. "Hey!" he said.

But the sound was barely a squeak. He hadn't used his voice in so long. He swallowed and tried again. "Hey!"

Only slightly louder. Frustrated, he picked up a rock and threw it. It landed right at the man's feet. He looked up, weapon raised. Cash raised his hands. "Don't shoot!" he pleaded.

"Cash!"

The woman was the one who said his name. He shifted his gaze, and looked into the astonished face of his aunt Rebecca. "Cash," she said again, and ran up the trail toward him.

Chapter Nineteen

Rebecca rushed forward to embrace Cash. It was really him. Safe. Alive. She stepped back to look at him more closely, and fear gripped her anew. "What's wrong?" she asked. "What happened to you?" He was so thin and pale, not at all the vibrant young man she knew.

"I'll tell you in a little bit." He looked past her at Wes. "Are you a cop?"

"Deputy Wes Landry, Rayford County Sheriff's Department." Wes stepped forward and offered his hand.

Cash took it, but released it quickly. "We have to get out of here," he said. "There's a guy out here who's trying to kill me."

"Who is trying to kill you?" Rebecca's gaze shifted to his leg, and the bloodstained jeans. The shock of the sight made her queasy. "Cash, you're hurt!" She gripped him harder, as if he might vanish if she released her hold on him.

"It's not safe out here," Cash said, speaking to Wes.

"There's a kind of cave back here." He pointed along the ledge. "We can talk there. Or we could just head for your car." He eased out of Rebecca's grasp. "That would be better. Let's just get out of here."

"Do you know how to get back to the parking area from here?" Wes asked.

Cash shook his head. "I'm so disoriented. I don't know where I am most of the time." He licked his cracked lips. "Do you have any food on you?"

"I'm sorry. No," Wes said.

Cash looked past him. "I heard gunshots. Was someone shooting at you?"

"They were," Rebecca said. "But we never saw who. Cash, what is going on? What have you gotten yourself into?"

Wes took her arm. "He's right. We're too exposed here. Let's go to this cave and figure out our next step."

She wanted to demand Cash tell her everything, right this second, but the memory of those bullets, so close to them, propelled her forward. They followed Cash along the ledge to a rock overhang that formed a shallow cave. She wrinkled her nose at the stench of unwashed body and sickness. Cash sank down onto the floor and pulled a foil emergency blanket around him, his face drained of color.

She knelt beside him. "We've been looking for you for days," she said. "I've been so worried."

"I never meant to worry you."

"We found your truck in a ravine," Wes said.

"Below the parking area. And your phone sent a couple of texts from Colorado Springs."

Cash closed his eyes. For a moment Rebecca thought he had passed out. She leaned over and took his hand and cradled it in both of hers. His fingers were ice cold. "I'm okay," he said. He looked up at Wes. "I wondered what happened to my truck. I came back to the parking area and it was just…gone. And I thought I must have dropped my phone, running through the woods."

"Running from what?" Wes sat on the other side of Cash, facing him.

Cash sighed. "It's a long story. Let me think a minute how to tell it."

"Payson Fritsch told us some things," Wes said. "About the meeting with Bart Smith, and about how he and Basher Monroe and you followed Smith to County Road 361."

"That's how it started," Cash said. "Smith was acting so strange. Basher and I were sure he was involved in something illegal. Probably drugs." He looked Wes in the eye. "You probably already know I had trouble with drugs. Basher had, too, so we knew a little bit about the kind of people who prey on others and get them hooked. I didn't want that happening to someone like Payson, or even younger kids, so I decided we should check this out."

"You should have gone to the sheriff with your suspicions," Rebecca said.

"I didn't have any proof," Cash said. "I wasn't

going to confront him or anything, just follow and see where he went." He rubbed the side of his neck. "How is Basher? Didn't he tell you any of this?"

Rebecca's throat tightened. She squeezed Cash's hand. "Honey, Basher is dead," she said. "Someone shot him."

His face twisted. "He told me he wasn't hurt bad. He told me all he needed to do was rest. I never should have left him."

"Who shot Basher?" Wes asked.

"That old miner. Or at least I think it was him." He pulled the emergency blanket more tightly around him.

"What happened?" Wes asked. "How did Martin Kramer come to shoot Basher?"

"I'll see if I can remember everything straight. So much has happened."

Rebecca listened, enthralled and horrified, as Cash took them through everything that had happened since she had seen him last and how he and Basher had decided Martin Kramer was the most likely person to be masquerading as Bart Smith.

Cash hunched forward, his face more animated. "It was the perfect setup. You could be doing anything down in that old mine. Later, toward dark, we came back and parked at the parking area at the start of the Jeep trail and hiked back to a place above the mine entrance. We had a good view and figured we'd watch for a while, but the place looked deserted, so we decided to go down and look closer. But this old guy came out with a shotgun and we ran away. Only Basher was shot."

He fell silent and Rebecca squeezed his hand again. "The wound didn't look that bad," Cash said. "It wasn't even bleeding much."

"Just one wound?" Wes asked. "Kramer shot Basher once?"

Cash nodded. "In his side. Why? Is that important?"

"Basher was shot in the head also," Wes said. "But after he was dead. Do you know anything about that?"

"No! That…that's sick." He cradled his head in his hands. "I should have stayed with him, but he insisted he would be fine on his own."

"Did anyone follow you back to Basher's place?" Wes asked.

"No. At least—I don't think so. I mean, I was pretty freaked out and focused on Basher, so I guess someone could have." He shook his head. "I don't know."

"What happened next?" Wes asked.

"Right. Well, I went back home —to Aunt Rebecca's house. I took a shower, and changed clothes, and spent most of the night tossing and turning, thinking about everything. The more I thought, the more I was sure there was something not right at that mine. Drug dealers get really paranoid because they know if anyone finds out what they're doing, they could end up in prison for a really long time or even dead. So I decided to make one more attempt to get some proof that the old guy was up to no good. Then I could bring that proof to you guys."

He told them about approaching the mine a second time and getting shot himself.

He looked down at the wound in his thigh. "I tried to find my truck, but it was just…gone. Then I realized I must have dropped my phone. I was scared, and I'd lost a lot of blood. I still had my pack, so I decided I'd better find someplace to hide. I found a cave—not this place, but another deeper cave. I holed up in there. I had some water and some energy bars and stuff. I kept drifting in and out. But finally I started to feel better and decided to try to make my way to a road or a house. Someplace I could call for help." He met Rebecca's gaze. "I knew you'd be worried. I figured you'd have people looking for me."

"I did," she said. "Lots of people looked for you. I don't understand why they didn't find you."

"There's a lot of territory out here," Wes said. "It's hard to cover it all. How did you end up here?"

As he told them about leaving the cave and searching for help, Rebecca could scarcely believe all he had been through. "Finally a white SUV stopped for me. I asked the driver to take me to the medical clinic where Aunt Rebecca works, but instead he took me back to that same parking area. He ordered me out of the truck, then he pulled out a big pistol. I didn't have any choice but to run again."

"What did he look like?" Wes asked. "Did he give you a name?"

"I can't be sure," Cash said. "But now that I've had time to think about it, I wonder if it was Bart Smith. Payson told you about the cheesy disguise Smith was wearing, right? The wig and the wild shirt?"

Wes nodded.

"I think this guy was wearing a disguise, too. Instead of a wig, he didn't have any hair at all—but I think it was one of those bald cap things actors use. I thought I could see the line below his hat. He had a big mustache, too. Really big, like a cartoon mustache, really black, with curled up ends. He had on dark glasses and his cheeks were really full and he spoke with a lisp like he had something stuffed in his cheeks. And he was wearing leather gloves so I never saw his hands. He didn't tell me his name or say much of anything, really. Except, when we got to the parking area, he said I needed to learn they don't like trespassers around here."

"When was this?" Wes asked.

"Yesterday," Cash said. "I ran blindly until I couldn't run anymore, then I realized I was really lost. I found this place to hide out and tried to think what to do next. I kept hoping someone would find me—someone who didn't want me dead."

"You say he threatened you with a handgun," Wes said.

"Yes. I thought maybe he was the one shooting at you just now."

"Those shots didn't come from a handgun," Wes

said. "And it wasn't a shotgun, like the miner, Martin Kramer, shot Basher with. This was a rifle."

Cash buried his head in his hand. "Maybe there are three of them. Maybe they're working together."

Rebecca slid her hand up his arm. Whereas his fingers were icy, the rest of him was hot to the touch. "Cash, I need to look at that gunshot wound," she said.

"What are you going to do about it?" he asked.

"I haven't worked in medical clinic for eight years without learning a little bit," she said. "I want to see it."

He said nothing, but lay on his side and shoved off the emergency blanket. Rebecca steeled herself, then pushed down the bloody pants and studied the angry swelling at his thigh. "It's infected," she said.

"I figured," he said.

She pressed gingerly around the wound and he flinched. She gave up and covered him again. "We need to get you out of here," she said.

"You should stay here with Cash while I try to make it back to the truck," Wes said. "I can try to radio for help. If the radio doesn't work, he can head to the Olsens' place at the yurt."

"How are you going to make it back there?" she asked. "And if you do, how are you going to find us again?"

He pulled out his phone. "I was stupid not to think of it before," he said. "The internal GPS will work without cell service. I can figure our location with it and use the information to get back to you. And there's internal mapping software that will help me find the truck. It's not precise, but it should be enough. If I get back to the road, I can make it from there on my own."

She opened her mouth to protest they should all go together. But Cash clutched her arm. "Let him go," he said. "I don't think I have the strength to walk out of here and I'm scared I'll die if you leave me alone."

"You're not going to die." She gripped his hand again. "Of course I'll stay with you."

"Come see me off," Wes said and held out his hand. She took it and he pulled her to her feet and they walked together out onto the ledge.

Once outside, he unholstered his pistol and pressed it into her hand. "Take this, but don't use it unless you have to."

She looked down at the weapon, heavy and cold against her skin. The thought that she might need this sent a tremor through her, but she forced back the fear and slipped the gun into her pocket. "All right."

Wes pulled her close and kissed her, hard. "I love you," he said.

And then he was gone, his words and the emotion behind them leaving her lightheaded. "I love you, too," she whispered, even though she knew he couldn't hear.

WES HALF SLID down the steep slope they had climbed to reach Cash's shelter, praying that what he'd once been told about the GPS on his phone would work in real life. Cash had looked to be in pretty bad shape; he didn't have time to waste.

He worried, too, about the person who had been shooting at them earlier. Whoever it was might track them to that cave, where Rebecca and Cash would be trapped. Try as he might, he couldn't sort out the different players in this drama. There was Kramer, who he was convinced had fired the shot that killed Basher Monroe. A ballistics test would prove that, and Kramer had admitted to firing on trespassers before.

But who was Bart Smith? A bizarre alter ego for Kramer? Someone working with Kramer? Another shady associate of Trey Allerton, who had a record of palling around with murderers?

He forced himself to focus on the map on his phone, though walking a straight line in this terrain proved difficult. He repeatedly had to detour around fallen trees, impenetrable thickets, or brush, or large rock outcroppings. But he pushed forward, moving as quickly as he could, the knowledge that Rebecca and Cash were depending on him keeping him going.

After an hour of walking, he reached the Jeep trail. The trail itself showed as a thin blue line on the map on his phone. He broke into a jog and a few minutes later, the parking lot was in sight.

His SUV listed to one side like a foundering ship, the back windshield spiderwebbed, spilling pellets of green safety glass across the bumper. Wes approached cautiously, every nerve alert. The sight of the wrecked SUV emphasized how isolated he was in this spot. But after watching the wrecked vehicle for several minutes, he decided he was spooking himself. He couldn't waste any more time. He dug out his keys and hit the button to unlock the door, then slipped inside and picked up the radio microphone.

Static crackled from the speakers when he first turned it on. He held the microphone close and spoke loudly. "This is Unit Nine. Do you copy?"

More static, but he thought he could almost make out a voice. "This is Unit Nine," he repeated.

No answer. He tried several more times, then tossed the mike down on the seat in disgust. Maybe someone on the other end had heard him, but he couldn't count on it. He needed to get moving again. If the Olsens were home, he'd send them to town for help while he took food and water back to Rebecca and Cash.

He slid out of the SUV and slammed the door behind him, sending another cascade of broken glass to the ground. He turned to walk away, just as Martin Kramer stepped from behind a tree and pointed a shotgun. "Don't move another muscle!" Kramer ordered.

Wes eased both hands into the air. "What are you doing, Mr. Kramer?"

"I came to get back the gold you stole." Kramer took a step forward. "And don't lie to me or I'll blow you away."

Chapter Twenty

Rebecca sat with Cash, the weight of Wes's pistol heavy against her hip, tension tightening every muscle. She wanted to ask Cash how he was feeling, but she also wanted him to sleep if he was able. So she remained quiet, listening to him breathe, reminding herself that as long as she could still hear him, then he was still with her. He still had a chance.

"Tell me about the cop." Cash's voice was raspy but startling in the silence.

"Do you mean Wes?" She shifted to face him. His eyes were closed, the blond beard fuzzing his jaw and the lines of pain around his eyes making him look much older.

More like his father, she realized with a start.

"Yeah. How'd you meet him?"

"We met when I reported you missing."

"Huh. Then I guess you can thank me later."

Now he sounded like Scott, that breezy sarcasm that had driven her crazy when he was alive, but that she had missed so keenly when he was gone. "Wes has been a big help," she said.

"He loves you, you know."

Had Cash heard their whispered exchange outside the cave? No, that wasn't possible. "What makes you say that?" she asked.

"I can tell. The way he touched your shoulder."

"How old are you again?"

"Old enough to know love when I see it. I'm happy for you. I never could figure out what you were doing alone."

"Because that would be the worst thing ever," she said.

"Yeah, well, I heard about you and Garrett. For what it's worth, I think he regrets dumping you. Though you should count yourself lucky. He and Dad may have been friends, but they're nothing alike. And that's not just my opinion—everyone says so."

She shouldn't have been surprised. The climbing community was tight, and there were no real secrets. She was curious about what people had said about her and Garrett, but she didn't want to know enough to hear it from Cash. That was all ancient history now, anyway. "You're right," she said. "Garrett is nothing like Scott." She put her hand on his arm. "But you're so much like your dad."

He turned his face away. Talking about his father had always been hard for him, though she suspected Cash thought about Scott all the time. She certainly did.

"If I get out of here alive, I'm going to go back to

California and go to college," he said. "I'll study counseling, or teaching, or something where I can make a difference. I'll still climb and teach climbing, but I want to do more."

"You're going to be okay," she said.

"Without me in the house, maybe your cop can move in," he said.

"Cash!"

"I'm just saying."

She laughed. In spite of everything, she laughed and felt lifted up by the release of tension. None of them knew what the future held, but it was so freeing to envision a positive tomorrow, instead of one where all the worst things happened.

"Someone's coming," Cash said and shoved up onto his elbows.

At first, she didn't hear anything, then she made out a sound like someone breathing hard and shoes scraping the loose rock on the slope leading up to their shelter. Heart thudding, she stood and slipped her hand into her pocket, touching the grip of the Glock.

"It's too soon for Wes to be back," Cash whispered.

She nodded and moved carefully toward the opening of the overhang. Whoever was out there moved closer. Rebecca slid the Glock from her pocket and steadied it with both hands.

The man came into view—a big man, with broad shoulders. He wore a black-knit beanie pulled down low, and if he had hair, it didn't show. Big dark glasses obscured his eyes, and he had a bright bandanna knotted around his throat and an extravagant black mustache. He grinned and held up his hands. "Hey now, don't shoot! I'm here to help."

"Don't come any closer," she said.

"I wouldn't dream of it." He slowly lowered his hands. "But I ran into a friend of yours—a sheriff's deputy—and he told me you and that lost climber were back in here and needed help, so I came to see what I could do."

"He's lying. That's the man who tried to kill me."

Rebecca glanced around, to where Cash leaned against the opening of their shelter. He had to cling to the rock to stay upright. "Cash, go back—" she began.

Then the breath was knocked from her as the stranger tackled her. He knocked the Glock from her hand and straddled her, crushing her with his weight. "I know you're only trying to protect the kid," he said. "I can appreciate that. So I'll do you a favor and I'll kill you first, before I shut him up for good."

"We haven't done anything to you!" she protested.

"That kid knows things I can't let become public knowledge," the man said. He drew a pistol from his side and pointed it toward Cash. "Don't try anything, unless you want your poor aunt to have to watch you die."

WES WATCHED KRAMER CAREFULLY. The older man's face was red, his eyes glittering with excitement—or rage. "I don't know what you're talking about," Wes said. "I haven't taken anything that belongs to you."

"Don't lie to me." Kramer kept the shotgun fixed on Wes. A ballistics vest probably wouldn't do much good against a shotgun slug fired at this distance. "I got home from the hospital and I could see your tracks in my driveway. And you were foolish enough to leave one of your cards where I had the gold stashed."

"I did stop by your place," Wes said. "I'd heard you'd been hurt and I wanted to check on you." Better to leave Rebecca out of this. "And I wanted to hear more about your accident. I think you're right that someone planted that piece of glass where you were likely to hurt yourself."

"You probably planted it there. That woman at the clinic—the one who was asking so many questions—probably let you know I had to go to the hospital, and you took the opportunity to swoop in and take everything I've worked for over the last five years. I'm not going to let you get away with it." He pumped the shotgun, the *ka-chunk* of the barrel sending a chill through Wes. "Now, hand it over."

"Put the gun down, Kramer," Wes ordered. "You've got bigger things to worry about than some missing gold. One of the young men you shot has died and the other one is in bad shape. You could be facing a murder charge."

"It's not murder if a man's defending his own property," Kramer said. "I told you I'd been having trouble with people coming around my place, trespassing and causing trouble. You didn't do anything about it, so

I had to. Besides, how do you know I'm the one who shot them?"

"We'll match the slugs to your shotgun," Wes said.

"Or maybe you won't be around to do that." Kramer brought the shotgun to his shoulder.

"Don't shoot!" Wes spoke loudly, freezing Kramer. "I'll give you back the gold," he added, when Kramer lowered the shotgun.

"I knew you were lying," Kramer said. "Where is it?"

"It's in the back of the SUV here." It took everything in Wes to turn his back on a man with a shotgun aimed at him, but he was counting on Kramer being more focused on the gold.

"What happened to your vehicle?" Kramer asked. "Looks like somebody shot it to pieces."

"I thought you did that," Wes said.

"Not me. I just got here a few minutes before you did. Now quit stalling and give me that gold."

Wes opened the rear lift gate of the SUV, sending a shower of broken glass over himself and the surrounding gravel. Glass crunched under his feet as he leaned into the vehicle and grabbed the first thing that came to hand—a duffel bag filled with tools for dealing with traffic accidents—flares, cones and other supplies. It was heavy and awkward, but he mustered every bit of energy to drag the bag from the vehicle and swing it toward Kramer. He hit the older man square in the chest, knocking him off balance. The shotgun slid to the ground and Kramer stumbled backward. Wes kicked the gun out of the way and leaped on the older man.

Kramer struggled out from under the duffel and grappled with Wes, grunting with the effort. Though he was almost thirty years older than Wes, years of work in the mine had hardened him, and anger added to his strength. The two rolled on the ground, Wes dodging a punch for every one he landed. He was dimly aware of the edge of the ravine somewhere beyond the front bumper of his SUV, and the still-cocked shotgun nearby as well.

Kramer swore and cuffed Wes hard on the side of the head. Wes shook off the dizziness and twisted one arm behind Kramer's back. He managed to flip the older man over and straddle him. From there he was able to restrain Kramer's hands behind his back. The older man continued to thrash beneath him, filling the air with abuse.

Wes climbed off Kramer and stood. "I don't have your gold," he said. He picked up the shotgun and carried it with him to the front of the SUV, and reached for the radio mike again. "Dispatch, this is Unit Nine. Officer needs assistance." He'd keep sending that message until someone answered or he'd rested enough to march Kramer to the nearest telephone.

CASH STARED AT the man with the gun—the same man who had given him a ride, then tried to shoot him—Bart Smith, or whatever his real name was. Looking for him had started this whole sorry escapade. Having him show up now, when he was so close to getting out of this alive, was too much.

Anger rose in his throat—a rage stronger than the fatigue and weakness that made even standing up a challenge. He clenched his fists at his side. He wasn't going to let this man—this stranger who Cash had done nothing to—ruin his life and his aunt's life. "What kind of idiot are you!" he shouted. "Why do you want to kill two people who never did anything to you?"

Aunt Rebecca's eyes widened and she shook her head, probably trying to warn him not to make this man any angrier than he already was. But Cash didn't care. He had had enough. "You're sick, you know that!" he said. "Why hurt someone you don't even know?"

"You're just an innocent kid, right?"

Bart smirked. "But you know enough about me and my business to put me away for a long time. And I can't let that happen." He aimed the pistol at Cash. "I should shut you up first, then deal with your aunt."

"Wes, no! Get back!" Rebecca shouted and waved her hands, staring over Bart's shoulder. Cash turned to look and saw nothing. Bart turned, too, and it was enough for Cash to take his chance. He charged the bigger, older man, driving his head into Smith's stomach, and knocked him off balance. Rebecca picked up the pistol she had dropped earlier and fired. The bullet missed Smith and Cash, but it apparently made Smith think twice about dealing with her. He shoved Cash off him and leaped from the ledge outside their shelter to the ground below, and took off running. They could hear him crashing through the woods for a long time after he disappeared from sight.

Rebecca sank to her knees, still clutching the gun in both hands. Cash crawled to her. "Are you okay?" he asked.

She nodded but said nothing, still clutching the gun.

"I think you can put the gun down now," Cash said. She was making him nervous, her finger hovering so near the trigger.

She nodded. "Right." And she slowly lowered the gun to her lap.

They sat side by side on the dirt floor of the rock overhang. Cash prayed Smith wouldn't return. He didn't know if he had the strength to stand. It was taking everything he had not to pass out.

They didn't say anything for a very long time. An hour, or maybe longer. Cash wasn't doing a good job of keeping track of time. He had fallen asleep, or maybe lost consciousness, when Rebecca nudged him. "Someone's coming," she said in a harsh whisper.

He raised his head. Someone was definitely walking toward their shelter, and not even trying to be quiet about it. "Rebecca! It's Wes!" a man shouted.

She cried out and dropped the gun, then stood and stumbled toward the opening of their shelter. Wes climbed over the side and gathered her to him as she sobbed against him. "It's going to be okay," he said.

"Help is right behind me. It was Kramer shooting at us, and he's under arrest and on his way to jail now."

"It wasn't Kramer," Cash said. "It was Bart Smith. He was here. He tried to kill us, but Aunt Rebecca shot at him and he ran away."

Wes looked from Cash to Rebecca. She nodded. "He was wearing the same disguise as the man who picked up Cash and tried to shoot him. He said Cash knew things about him that would ruin him, and that he was going to kill us both."

"But I don't know anything about him," Cash said. "I don't even know who he really is."

"What's this about Kramer?" Rebecca asked.

"He was waiting at my SUV and held a gun on me. He accused me of stealing his gold. There was a bit of a struggle, but he's under arrest now."

"Are you all right?" She clutched at his shoulders.

"I'm fine." He looked at Cash. "They're sending a helicopter to get you out of here," he said. "It should be here soon. I've got some fellow deputies arranging a landing spot not far from here."

"Thanks." Cash lowered himself to the ground again. Running at Smith had taken everything out of him. That chopper couldn't get here soon enough.

He closed his eyes and drifted off, though he had a fleeting impression of his aunt Rebecca and Wes, kissing as if they might never stop.

WES HATED TO leave Rebecca to deal with Cash on her own, but he had to get to work putting together the pieces of the case. "Go and do your job," she urged him. "It's more important to me that you find the people who hurt Cash than that you sit with me in a hospital waiting room."

"Keep me posted." He kissed her again, then whispered, "I love you."

"I love you, too," she said and the words made him feel a foot taller than he had before.

When he returned to the scene, Gage caught him up with developments so far. "Kramer has contacted a lawyer and we're waiting to question him, but he's had plenty to say about his stolen gold. Seems he's been stashing away the proceeds from his mine for several years and has accumulated a small fortune. He alternates between believing you stole it or that Cash and his friends—he doesn't say who that might be—spirited it away."

"Cash says he and Basher never got close enough to see much of anything," Wes said. "They thought Kramer was manufacturing or distributing drugs."

"No sign of that," Gage said. "And no sign of your mysterious bald-headed, mustachioed attacker, either. We were able to get a tracking dog on loan from the Colorado Bureau of Investigation, and they're out with a team, trying to find him, but no luck so far."

"I want to talk to Trey Allerton," Wes said.

"I agree," Gage said. "He has a habit of being on the periphery whenever anything bad happens around here."

Allerton was more affable than usual when he answered their knock that afternoon. "I was thinking about calling the station and asking what's with all the cop cars going up and down the road all afternoon," he said.

"May we come in?" Wes asked.

In answer, Allerton held the door open wide.

Courtney Baker was sitting on the sofa with her daughter, Ashlyn, in her lap. "Is something wrong?" she asked when Wes and Gage entered.

"Martin Kramer has been arrested for the murder of Basher Monroe." Wes had debated which topic to lead with and had decided on this one.

"I'm not surprised," Allerton said. "The old guy threatened to shoot anyone who set foot on his property."

"We've determined Kramer fired the shot that killed Basher Monroe, but someone else shot Basher in the head, after he was already dead at his camper," Wes said. "Do you know anything about that?"

"No. Why would I? I never met Basher Monroe."

"Kramer says someone stole a cache of gold he'd been saving up," Gage said. "Do you know anything about that?"

Allerton laughed. "So the old man really had gold? Are you sure he's not making that up?"

"Did you know about the gold?" Gage pressed.

"No way. And I still don't believe he ever found enough to amount to anything. Though I guess from the crime scene van I saw headed his way, y'all think Kramer is hiding something."

"Cash Whitlow was found this afternoon," Wes said. He watched for a reaction from Allerton, but the handsome face remained impassive.

"Dead or alive?" Allerton asked.

"He's alive," Wes said. "He's expected to make a full recovery."

Courtney looked up. "That's so wonderful. I'm glad."

"Yeah, good to hear," Allerton said. "Of course, I imagine he's pretty traumatized. Bound to be."

"We're looking for another man who attacked Cash," Wes said. "A big guy, bald, with a thick black mustache."

Allerton shook his head. "I don't know anyone like that."

"Maybe you've seen him. He picked up Cash when he was walking down this road yesterday, and pursued him again this afternoon."

"I was gone all day yesterday and most of today," Allerton said. "You can ask Courtney."

"We were together all day yesterday and today," Courtney said. She didn't look at Wes or Gage, focused instead on her daughter. "We didn't get home until a little while ago."

Allerton stood. "Sorry we can't be of more help," he said. "But it's getting late, so I'll say good night."

Wes wanted to press him, but doubted he'd get anything more. "What do you think?" he asked Gage when the two of them were back in Gage's SUV, headed to town.

"I think we don't have any evidence against Allerton. We'll keep looking for Bart Smith, but for now we'll have to content ourselves with a resolution to the murder of Basher Monroe and Cash Whitlow home safe." He glanced at Wes. "Not a bad day's work."

It wasn't, but Wes hated loose ends. Unfortunately there were almost always loose ends in any case.

It was after eight o'clock by the time he got to the hospital in Junction, where Cash had been flown for treatment. He found Rebecca with Cash in a private room on the surgical floor. Despite having undergone surgery to remove a shotgun slug from his thigh, and treatment for exposure and an infection, the young man already looked better. "Hey," he answered Wes's greeting, almost shyly.

Rebecca stood and embraced him. "Cash is doing so well," she said.

"Good to hear it," he said.

"So are you here on business or pleasure?" Cash asked, then grinned at Rebecca.

"A little of both." He held up a folder he'd brought with him. "Can you look at a few pictures for me? See if you recognize anyone?"

"Sure." Cash sat up a little straighter, wincing only a little.

Wes looked at Rebecca. "Any reason I shouldn't do this? Do they have him on heavy-duty pain meds?"

"No pain meds," Cash said.

Wes's surprise must have shown, because Cash added, "I didn't want to risk getting hooked on opiates again. I'm okay with over-the-counter meds. I feel so much better already than I did in the woods. I got to eat a bowl of soup for dinner. Tomorrow I might graduate to real food—a hamburger."

"Fair enough." Wes slid the folder onto the tray table in front of Cash. "Just tell me if anyone looks familiar." He had pulled together photographs of men who fit the description of Bart Smith, with and without hair, with and without a mustache. A photo of Trey Allerton was in the mix, too."

Cash studied the photographs for a long while. Rebecca stood beside him, looking over his shoulder. Finally he pushed the folder away. "Sorry," he said. "I don't recognized anyone."

"No need to apologize." Wes turned to Rebecca. "What about you?"

She shook her head. "None of them are the man I remember."

He nodded and closed the folder. "We're not having any luck finding Bart Smith," he said. "He may have left the area. Until we know for sure, we're going to be keeping a close eye on both of you. If you see anyone acting suspicious, or you feel threatened, or just uneasy, let me know right away."

"That's good," Cash said. "But when I get out of here, I've already decided I'm going back to California. I figure you'll do a good job of looking after Aunt Rebecca, and you'd probably just as soon not have me around, cramping your style."

"Cash!" Rebecca's cheeks flushed pink.

Wes put his arm around her shoulders. "I promise to take good care of your aunt," he told Cash.

Cash nodded.

A nurse came in. "Time for a wound check," she said.

Rebecca walked with Wes into the hallway. "I'm sorry we haven't found Bart Smith," he said. "We'll keep searching, but we'll need to get lucky to track him down. So far we haven't come up with any hint of who he really is or where he might be hiding. Search and Rescue are pretty sure he's not still in the woods. The search dog led them to a place where a vehicle had been parked. They think he probably drove away in it."

"It's okay," she said. "You know who killed Basher Monroe, and you found Cash. That's what matters most."

"You found Cash. If not for you, I probably wouldn't have gone back out there to look for him again."

She glanced back at the closed door to Cash's room. "I think Cash saved my life," she said. "I pretended you were coming in order to distract Bart Smith, or whoever he was, and Cash ran at him, knocking him over. Then I fired your gun. I didn't come close to hitting him, but he ran off anyway."

"He's a remarkable young man. And you're a remarkable woman." He tugged her toward an alcove at the end of the hallway, where they would have more privacy. "I meant what I said about protecting you. Not just now, but for the long-term. For forever."

Her breath caught, and she search his face. "What are you saying?"

He took a deep breath. Was he being rash? Rushing her? "Rebecca, will you marry me?" he asked. "I don't have a ring, and I didn't plan an elaborate proposal, I'm just saying what's in my heart. I love you, and I want to be with you. Forever."

"It's what's in my heart too," she said. She kissed him, very lightly, then drew back. "Yes."

"It's not too soon?" he asked. "We haven't known each other very long."

"I've been waiting for you for years," she said and kissed him again. "What took you so long to get here?"

He could have told her that they both needed to go through all the things they went through to get to be the people they were today, able to promise to love each other and mean it. But he didn't waste the words. He only held her tight, and promised himself that he was going to stop wishing to change the past and focus on the future. With this woman, in this place.

Exactly where he was supposed to be.

* * * * *

Don't miss the conclusion
of Cindi Myers's miniseries,
Eagle Mountain: Search for Suspects,
when Standoff at Grizzly Creek
goes on sale next month.

You'll find it wherever
Harlequin Intrigue books are sold!

#2061 MURDER GONE COLD
A Colt Brothers Investigation • by B.J. Daniels
When James Colt decides to solve his late father's final murder case, he has no idea it will implicate his high school crush Lorelei Wilkins's stepmother. Now James and Lorelei must unravel a cover-up involving some of the finest citizens of Lonesome, Montana...including a killer determined to keep the truth hidden.

#2062 DECOY TRAINING
K-9s on Patrol • by Caridad Piñeiro
Former marine Shane Adler's used to perilous situations. But he's stunned to find danger in the peaceful Idaho mountains—especially swirling around his beautiful dog trainer, Piper Lambert. It's up to Shane—and his loyal K-9 in training, Decoy—to make sure a mysterious enemy won't derail her new beginning...or his.

#2063 SETUP AT WHISKEY GULCH
The Outriders Series • by Elle James
After losing her fiancé to an IED explosion, sheriff's deputy Dallas Jones planned to start over in Whiskey Gulch. But when she finds herself in the middle of a murder investigation, Dallas partners with Outrider Levi Warren. Their investigation, riddled with gangs, drugs and death threats, sparks an unexpected attraction—one they may not survive.

#2064 GRIZZLY CREEK STANDOFF
Eagle Mountain: Search for Suspects • by Cindi Myers
When police deputy Ronin Doyle happens upon stunning Courtney Baker, he can't shake the feeling that something's not right. And as the lawman's engulfed by an investigation that rocks their serene community, more and more he's convinced that Courtney's boyfriend has swept her—and her beloved daughter—into something sinister...

#2065 ACCIDENTAL WITNESS
Heartland Heroes • by Julie Anne Lindsey
While searching for her missing roommate, Jen Jordan barely survives coming face-to-face with a gunman. Panicked, the headstrong mom enlists the help of Deputy Knox Winchester, her late fiancé's best friend, who will have to race against time to protect Jen and her baby...and expose the criminals putting all their lives in jeopardy.

#2066 GASLIGHTED IN COLORADO
by Cassie Miles
Deputy John Graystone vows to help Caroline McAllister recover her fractured memories of why she's covered in blood. As mounting evidence surrounds Caroline, a stalker arrives on the scene shooting from the shadows and leaving terrifying notes. Is John protecting—and falling for—an amnesiac victim being gaslighted...or is there more to this crime than he ever imagined?

*Bad things have been happening to Buckhorn residents,
and Darby Fulton's sure it has something to do with
a new store called Gossip. As a newspaper publisher,
she can't ignore the story, any more than she can resist
being drawn to former cop Jasper Cole.
Their investigation pulls them both into a twisted
scheme of revenge where secrets are a deadly weapon...*

Read on for a sneak preview of
Before Buckhorn,
part of the Buckhorn, Montana series,
by New York Times *bestselling author B.J. Daniels.*

Saturday evening the crows came. Jasper Cole looked
up from where he'd been standing in his ranch kitchen
cleaning up his dinner dishes. He'd heard the rustle of
feathers and looked up with a start to see several dozen
crows congregated on the telephone line outside.

Just the sight of them stirred a memory of a time
dozens of crows had come to his grandparents' farmhouse
when he was five. The chill he felt at both the memory
and the arrival of the crows had nothing to do with the
cool Montana spring air coming in through the kitchen
window.

He stared at the birds, noticing that they all seemed
to be watching him. There were so many of them, their
ebony bodies silhouetted against a cloudless sky, their

shiny dark eyes glittering in the growing twilight. As this murder of crows began to caw, he listened as if this time he might decode whatever they'd come to tell him. But like last time, he couldn't make sense of it. Was it another warning, one he was going to wish that he'd heeded?

Laughing to himself, he closed the window and finished his dishes. He didn't really believe the crows were a portent of what was to come this time—any more than last time. His grandmother had, though. He remembered watching her cross herself and mumble a prayer as if the crows were an omen of something sinister on its way. As it turned out, she'd been right.

At almost forty, Jasper could scoff all he wanted, even as a bad feeling settled deep in his belly. That feeling only worsened as the crows suddenly all took flight as if their work was done.

Over the next few days, he would remember the evening the crows appeared. It was the same day Leviathan Nash arrived in Buckhorn, Montana, to open his shop in the old carriage house and strange things had begun to happen—even before people started dying.

Don't miss
Before Buckhorn by B.J. Daniels,
available February 2022 wherever
HQN books and ebooks are sold.

HQNBooks.com

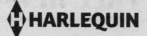

HARLEQUIN

Heartfelt or thrilling, passionate or uplifting—Harlequin is more than just happily-ever-after.

With twelve different series to choose from and new books available every month, you are sure to find stories that will move you, uplift you, inspire and delight you.

SIGN UP FOR THE HARLEQUIN NEWSLETTER
Be the first to hear about great new reads and exciting offers!

Harlequin.com/newsletters